# The Illusion

**Even the book morphs!
Flip the pages
and check it out!**

Look for other **ANIMORPHS**®
titles by K.A. Applegate:

*The Hork-Bajir Chronicles*

ALTERNAMORPHS
*The First Journey*

# ANIMORPHS®

## The Illusion

### K.A. Applegate

AN
**APPLE**
PAPERBACK

SCHOLASTIC INC.
New York Toronto London Auckland Sydney
Mexico City New Delhi Hong Kong

Cover illustration by David B. Mattingly

ISBN 0-439-07033-3

12 11 10 9 8 7 6 5 4 3 2 1          9/9 0 1 2 3 4/0

Printed in the U.S.A.
First Scholastic printing, September 1999

The author wishes to thank Ellen Geroux for her help in preparing this manuscript.

And for Michael and Jake

# The Illusion

# CHAPTER 1

My name is Tobias.

And I don't think I could have felt more uncomfortable if I'd just been asked to give an impromptu speech on the French Revolution in front of an all-school assembly.

Well, okay. I guess that would be pretty bad. But this Friday night was definitely right up there.

Back when I was a regular kid, school dances made me a little uneasy. I've always been a loner and all, and they just weren't my thing. But now! Now that I spent most of my life as a red-tailed hawk — hunting, flying, protecting my meadow — dances made me feel even weirder.

Bird-boy at the ball.

1

Why had I let Rachel talk me into this? I mean, what do you do with your arms? They just dangled there. Stiff. Awkward. And my eyes! I'd fix a stare on someone and forget, until it was too late, that people tend not to do that. A big, burly redhead noticed as the raptor in me burned a hole through his girlfriend.

"Jerk!"

Oops. Hard to remember I wasn't perched in a tree a half mile away.

I'd been cool enough at the last school dance. That was more of a group thing, I guess. Tonight it was . . . I don't know . . . a date? No, no, no. We were all there. Pretending to be acquaintances.

I looked ridiculous, I was sure of it. And I was sure that everyone else thought so, too.

Did Rachel?

I glanced at her. She seemed impatient. Angry almost, as she surveyed the dimly lit gym in an absent yet determined way. They'd taped some helium balloons to the bleachers and draped strings of multicolored lights from the basketball hoops. We were down at the far end next to the deejay. So close to the speaker my eardrums were numb.

Rachel was as beautiful as ever. Really. I mean I wouldn't tell her this, but she made the other girls look pretty plain. Her gold hair gleamed in the strobe light. Her bright eyes caught mine. I knew she wanted me to dance with her. I just couldn't do it. My human body was sweating. I felt confined. I needed air. I looked away.

Did I mention that my name is Tobias?

Just Tobias. Even if it were safe to tell you my last name, I'm not sure I'd know what to say. Whether it would be a human name, an Andalite name, or just "hawk." I don't know. Because, see, I'm a little of each.

"Let's kick it, boys and girls!"

My friend Marco, unlike me, was in paradise. He was belting out lyrics like his first name was "Ice" or something.

He slide-stepped toward us, spun around, and stopped, squealing his sneaker on the gym floor. He froze with one finger pointed at me and one at Rachel.

She glared at him. "Some kind of chemical imbalance, Marco?"

"Hah. Hah. And also, a bonus, hah." He grinned. "This is a natural high. A good music high. A lots-of-girls-in-short-skirts high. A people laughing high. This is fun. Do you two remember fun?"

Rachel caught my eye again. Again I looked away, up at the clock. Twenty minutes left in morph. Not much time.

3

"You need to cut loose, my friends," Marco continued in a meaningful tone. "It's all about rhythm. You gotta commune with the rhythm, step inside the beat."

"Look, Marco, go work your magic somewhere else," Rachel snapped.

"Okay. Which proves what I've always known: Neither of you is any fun, and together, even less. I'll just have to find my own party. Later."

I had too much on my mind. So much to take in. Lights. Music. A lot of songs I didn't even recognize. I'd been gone too long.

"Listen, Rachel, I have to get going. And," I added more quietly, "time's running out."

"What do you mean? You have a full, well, at least fifteen minutes left. You saying you'd rather be sitting up in your tree, watching owls eat nocturnal rodents, than be with me?" she asked. Her tone was somewhere between challenging and coy. Dangerous in either direction.

"Well, no, of course not. I mean, not exactly."

"What?"

"It's just all these other people. The noise. This body . . ." I looked around, worried that someone might overhear. But no, not with human ears, not with this much noise.

"You mean your body. The body you're in now is your body, Tobias. It's who you truly are. Normally, naturally."

4

We'd been through this before. I didn't know how to answer. And I didn't know why she was pushing it.

Ever since I overstayed the two-hour time limit in morph I've considered hawk to be my true form. Hawk is the body I have to keep if I want to help the other Animorphs and Ax combat the Yeerk invasion. Why was Rachel ignoring reality? She knew as well as anyone that I'd be out of the fight if I stayed more than two hours in human form.

All of which must sound strange. Possibly insane. So let me back up.

Here's the situation: The human race is under attack by a cruel and scheming enemy. As you're reading this, the parasitic alien species called Yeerks continues to enslave human minds. Armed with a capability you can't even imagine till you've seen it in action, the Yeerks wrest from us the one thing we hold most dear: free will.

Once one of these slimy, gray, sluglike parasites squirms into your ear canal, and melds and shapes itself to all the crevices of your brain, it controls you. That's right. It dictates your every thought. Your every move! The Yeerks have created an army by infesting and controlling alien races.

Gedds. Taxxons. Hork-Bajir.

Humans.

By secretly infiltrating our society, the Yeerks have become a nearly undefeatable enemy.

Who's fighting them? What's the human race's best and only hope in this war? A young Andalite cadet, along with five kids who call themselves the Animorphs because they alone, of all humans, possess a unique Andalite technology: the power to morph. To become any animal they can touch.

Ax, Jake, Cassie, Marco, Rachel. And me.

Together, we fight. But it can be a lonely war.

Because, see, morphing has some limitations. And one involves a time limit. Stay in morph longer than two hours and you're stuck in morph forever.

That's what happened to me. I was trapped as a redtailed hawk. A *nothlit,* as the Andalites call someone stuck in morph.

After many months, the powerful alien called the Ellimist gave me back my ability to morph. Even made it possible for me to morph into my former human body. I could choose to trap myself in my human form now, but I would lose my morphing power for good. Do you see? I would be useless. Unable to honor my responsibility to Earth, powerless to resist Yeerk evil.

"Just dance with me, Tobias. Please." A slow song started. I was surprised. I actually knew this one. Goo Goo Dolls. Couples filled up the dance

6

floor. Cassie and Jake were on the other side of the gym, swaying gently, arms around each other.

Rachel reached out and took my hand.

It's funny. We've been on so many missions together. Battled Hork-Bajir-Controllers side by side. Saved each other's lives time and again. And still, after all that, it's something as simple as dancing that makes my heart pound.

Out onto the dance floor. I slid my arms around her waist. Felt her hands on my neck.

I let myself relax. Something I can rarely do as a hawk and an Animorph. I gave myself over to the moment. Let the music's rhythm lull me into a waking dream.

We danced, turning slowly. As we turned, my eyes wandered to the darkened scoreboard up in the corner. Banners listing the school's team victories. The bleachers, where a balloon had just broken free and sailed toward the ceiling.

And then I saw . . . the clock.

# CHAPTER 2

The time!

I jerked away to get a better look. Human eyes are worthless for long distances.

Could the clock be right?

"Oh, God. Rachel. Eight minutes," I whispered wildly. "I have to get out of here."

"No, wait a minute. Stay."

"Stay? Rachel, have you lost it? I have to find a place to demorph. Now!"

I tried to stay calm, but ended up half-walking, half-running toward the door, brushing past a teacher I used to have for English, back when I was still in school. Mr. Feyroyan. He did a double take, but I was gone before he had the chance to remember me.

Down the locker-lined hallway I ran. Past my old science classrooms. Rachel was running right behind me. Had she seen the clock before I had? Had she known time was short and chosen not to tell me, hoping I'd forget? Hoping I'd be "accidentally" trapped in human morph? No. Of course not. She wouldn't want that. And yet . . . I wasn't completely sure.

"Wait up a second. Hey," she called, angrily.

I slowed and finally stopped in front of a bulletin board display. On birds of prey, of all things.

Tacked to the cork was the image of a bald eagle, wings spread wide, soaring in a deep blue sky. And a northern harrier on a fence post, silhouetted against the clouds. "Tobias, I want to explain . . ." She broke off as her eyes followed mine to the picture of the red-tailed hawk and the caption beneath it. "Longevity in the wild," it read. "Almost never reaches the figures attained by captive birds guarded against disease and predation. A generous estimate: eighteen years."

Rachel stared at the wall. I looked at the floor. In an instant, the bulletin board display had thrown our friendship into the harsh light of reality. Rachel was a girl who could, on occasion, become a bird of prey. I was a hawk who could, on occasion, become human.

Several big steps past being Montagues and

9

Capulets like Romeo and Juliet. Remaining hawk meant meals of still-living mice.

Rachel was in my face, now. Intense, words spilling out. "Look, the fight is important to us all, Tobias. So important to you that you've given up everything human to be a warrior. What am I even saying? You risk your life every day. I understand all that. I do. We're the same, you and me. Warriors."

She paused to consider her next words. She was embarrassed by what she was about to say. Fighting to get past her embarrassment. "But you've got to realize that there's more. I'm not just a warrior," she said, her blue eyes glittering so close to mine. "I'm a girl. I'm trying not to let myself be dragged off the cliff, away from all normalcy, into this insane life we live. I don't like what it does to me, Tobias, and I need to be a girl again. I need a little bit of normalcy, okay? Not a lot, but some."

She pushed back, away from me. I'd never seen Rachel so emotional. Unless, of course, the emotion was an act. Unless she was stalling me just to eat up the minutes, to trap me, to —

"All the things we're supposed to live while we're in school, Tobias, you know, dances like this, nights out at the movies, walks on the beach. That stuff is passing us by. I want those things. We deserve them. And if you were human . . ."

I cut her off, repeating her words out loud. "Yeah. If I were human. If."

So she'd finally said what I'd known she felt all along. It made sense. She was right. She did need normalcy. Rachel had gone pretty far out on the edge in this war.

But it still hurt. Hurt worse because I didn't have an answer.

"I need to go," I said flatly. I turned and walked hurriedly toward the T-shaped intersection, where the long hallway off the gym met an even larger corridor running from the front of the school to the rear. The hall was quiet, but populated. Kids leaning against the lockers. Talking. Hanging out.

My walk turned into a run. I didn't want to draw attention to myself, but I had to move! I rounded the corner. Almost free. The back exit was just at the end of this hallway.

"What the . . . !" I stopped suddenly. My escape was blocked by one of those collapsible metal gates that pull between walls.

"Stay cool," I mumbled to myself. With forced composure I sauntered back away from the gate as if I were just loitering, and headed the other way. The front entrance was my only choice.

Two or three steps out into the hall, I sensed someone else was there. I froze.

In front of orange-painted lockers, not fifteen feet away, stood Vice Principal Chapman. Controller. Nemesis.

He didn't see me because he wasn't alone. He was focused on the kid he'd cornered against the wall.

The kid? Erek King. Erek the Chee.

Rachel! I looked back at her. She was still in the hallway. I don't know how much alarm registered on my face. I'm pretty out of touch with facial expressions. But she obviously read the surprise in my eyes. She tiptoed to the corner and peered around.

"Oh, I know you, Erek," Chapman said with his Vice Principal Disciplinarian voice. "I know your face, all right. I've seen you at meetings of The Sharing. I'm just saying I saw you throw away a cigarette just now."

"No way, Mr. Chapman," Erek said, sounding exactly like the kid he was supposed to be.

"We don't need young men such as yourself smoking, especially not with the added attention. The media."

At one level it was funny. The idea that Erek, an android beneath the holographic exterior, would smoke. And the idea that Chapman, a powerful Controller, would care. Both of them were playing roles layered with deception.

What did Chapman mean, "especially now"?

Not my problem. Erek could take care of himself. He wasn't my concern. I had my own mess. I'd been out of school for a while, but there was the chance that Chapman would recognize me, too, start asking questions, get suspicious. I couldn't let him get a good look at me. But I had to pass him to get outside.

Slowly, very slowly, I retraced my steps till I stood next to Rachel, our backs pressed up against the lockers.

"Look, Rachel, I need your help," I whispered.

And that's when I heard someone call my name.

"Tobias!"

Mr. Fcyroyan waved a large, friendly hand as he strode toward us from the gym. His black curls bounced excitedly. His mouth opened to a broad smile. He had remembered me.

The clock was ticking down and I wasn't even sure Rachel was on my side.

In minutes I'd be trapped. Trapped as a person who was no longer me.

# CHAPTER 3

Rachel grabbed my arm. "Over the gate," she ordered. "There's no other way. I'll hold off Feyroyan. Meet you outside." For a second our eyes met. She flashed a hint of a smile.

I dashed around the corner. Dove at the metal gate. It clattered and crashed as I struggled to gain a foothold.

"Hey! Hey, get down from there! What do you think you're doing?" Chapman yelled. I was out of practice with this body. I was clumsy. But I was climbing.

And headed for the tiny space between the top of the gate and the ceiling. Hardly an opening at all, but it would have to be big enough. I gripped one square-edged metal link after the next.

"No, you're wrong." Feyroyan's voice bounced off the ceiling. "That's Tobias, I'm sure it is."

I brushed the top just as Chapman and Feyroyan reached the bottom. Chapman grabbed hold and the gate swayed.

"Son, listen to me. Get down from there!"

I hoisted myself up and through the gap. My chest scraped. I blew the air out of my lungs and pressed through the opening. My shirt caught a gate iron and held me. I thrashed. A shot of adrenaline hit me like a fist. The shirt ripped. I was free.

I scrambled down the opposite side and jumped to the floor, turning to run even before I landed.

I raced down the dim, empty hallway, footfalls pounding so fast the sound was nearly continuous. I wasn't running from Chapman. I wasn't running from Feyroyan, or the dance, or Rachel, or the raptor display. I was running for my life.

I dove at the panic bar, burst outside, and bounded across the field. Feet pummeled the earth. My chest heaved. The chill of night air enveloped me — night air that felt like home.

"Demorph!" I screamed inside my head. "Demorph now!" I focused. I willed it with all that was in me. I closed my eyes.

Nothing.

Still nothing.

Only my human body, my burning lungs, the throbbing pain from the scratch across my chest.

Nooo!

Wumpp. "Ahhh!"

Thud. "Ouch."

I tripped and slammed to the ground.

In the darkness not much was visible. A human arm against the dirt. Human fingers. And then!

All I could see was a lattice of feathers spreading across the skin of my hand. Finally!

My legs were shrinking, pulling and sucking up into my body. I felt my toes minimize, slowly fuse, then grow out again into eight ripping, deadly talons.

I looked toward the night sky, so relieved.

So happy.

And when, all at once, the brilliance and precision of hawk vision replaced fuzzy human sight, the number of stars multiplied. Hawk vision isn't worth much at night, it's true. Except for stargazing. All the dim little luminous points you can just barely make out as a human blaze into focus with hawk eyes.

"Tobias?"

I scrambled up, flapped my wings clumsily to steady myself.

Mr. Feyroyan's voice was more tentative now, uncertain. He stood alone in the middle of the playing field, searching for me in the shadows. He was one of the few friends I'd had when I was in school. He was a teacher, but he was young, and a dreamer. I'd always thought he was like an older me.

He gave up, and turned back toward the school.

I struggled with the shirt Rachel had picked out for me to wear to the dance. It was still buttoned around my hawk body. I tore at it with my beak, stabbed at it with my talons. Finally, I was clear of it.

It was tough to gain altitude in the cool air. I flapped hard and circled the school. No sign of Rachel. But I spotted Jake on the front steps. He was alone, thinking, I guess. Maybe just enjoying a minute of peace and quiet.

I swooped in low to land on the branch of a birch tree a few feet above him.

<Hey, Jake.>

He looked up. Jake's my age. But there are times when his eyes are the eyes of a tired old man. "Where have you been? Rachel said you were jammed. Guess you made it."

<Yeah.> I felt pained by the possibility that

17

Rachel might have been pulling for the time limit. <I made it. Where is Rachel?>

Jake shrugged. "Don't know. But that's the least of our problems. Before Chapman busted him, Erek gave me some bad news. I need you to find Ax. Tell him to meet us at the barn."

<Tonight?>

"Yes!" He stopped short. "No. I mean, no. We can't tonight. We've got parents waiting up for us. Better tomorrow morning. Saturday."

<No problem. But what's up?>

"It's the Anti-Morphing Ray," he said. "The Chee have lost track of it. I mean they've got nothing."

<Yeah? That's bad.> I was having a hard time tracking. My mind was still back with Rachel and a ticking clock.

"Erek says the Yeerks are ready to test it." He paused for a beat. "On a live subject."

He let that one hang in the air for a minute. We both knew what it meant. The AMR. The ultimate weapon. A ray that could force us out of morph. Make us revert to natural form. We'd tried once to destroy it. We'd lost.

Morphing was our only weapon. All we had. The Yeerks had to be stopped. No discussion.

"But how do you bust up a Yeerk plan when you don't know where to show up to —"

<Hold up,> I said.

Three chattering girls came out of the door and ran down the steps past Jake.

"Hi, Jake," one of them said.

"Yeah, hi, um . . . hi." He waved. The girl looked insulted. "Brittany!" Jake added, too late.

<Okay, we're clear,> I said.

Jake massaged his forehead with his fingers. "Man, I don't even know the people in my classes anymore."

<You are a little busy,> I said.

"Yeah. Look, find Ax. You and him, tomorrow, bright and early. We have to get on this."

<I'll be at the meeting tomorrow, Jake. I'll make sure Ax is there, too. But get some sleep, man, okay?>

"Oh, don't worry about me. I'm into catnaps. You know, like Napoleon did. Twenty minutes here, twenty there. Pretty soon you've slept eight hours and it hasn't even slowed you down." He stood up and leaned against the railing.

"I'm glad you made it, Tobias. You're our eyes. Our ears. Our air force. If we lost you we'd be nothing. Like Joan of Arc without her sword. Patton without his pearl-handled pistols . . ."

<Saddam without forty-eight palaces, the special Republican Guard, and a jar of anthrax? Stop the flattery, man. You're making me blush.> We both laughed. It felt good to hear Jake say I was indispensable. But with Jake you could

19

never be sure anymore what was sincere. And what was just expedient.

He'd been the most open of guys, back in the old days. What you saw with Jake was what you got. But he'd been a leader for a long time now. He'd learned to say what he needed to say.

Jake needed me as one of the Animorphs. He liked me, respected me, was happy for me when I was happy. And, when he had to, he used me without regard for anything but winning.

<Been boning up on famous leaders, haven't you?>

"A little, yeah. Don't tell anyone, though. I want my brilliance to appear unstudied. Natural." Jake smiled up at me and gave a quick salute. "Later, Red Baron."

<See you there, fearless leader.>

I took off and winged toward Ax's scoop on air that was welcoming and crisp.

# CHAPTER 4

Cassie's parents were gone for the day. Her mom was working at The Gardens. Her dad was at a vet conference.

I was up on the usual rafter, keeping a lookout just in case. We were waiting for Jake and most likely Erek.

Rachel was lounging on the hay bales, fighting to stay awake after a late night. Blue eyes appeared, disappeared, reappeared at half-mast.

Ax, in Andalite form, stood nearby, a bizarre mix of blue deer, stalk-eyed boy, and scorpion. Funny how we'd all gotten used to seeing a creature so utterly inhuman hanging around.

Cassie was preoccupied with a bald eagle, tending it even though she said it was living its

21

final days. It had fought a terminal illness, and lost. It was hard to look at it. Feathers matted. A patch missing from the chest. A noble creature at the end of its time. I shuddered at the thought.

"Let me get this straight," Marco said. "Erek got busted, not because he's an android walking the streets in a hologram shield. Not because he's an informant for the 'Andalite bandits.' But for smelling like cigarettes?"

"It was because Chapman knows he's a member of The Sharing," Rachel said. "Members aren't supposed to be troublesome. You know. More Boy Scouty than the Boy Scouts. Especially because they have this big thing going on, this new community center. There'll be media, there. Have to watch that image."

The Sharing is a Yeerk front organization. On the surface, a do-good, family-oriented get-together. Beneath that veneer, the Yeerks used the wholesome enticements as a means of recruiting Controllers.

<Igniting sticks of plant and paper?> Ax wondered. <Why is that such a serious offense?>

<Because cigarettes can kill you,> I answered. <That is, if a golden eagle or a case of coccidiosis doesn't get you first.>

Rachel gave me a dirty look. "So not funny."

"And because they become an addiction," Cassie said.

"Like Marco and computer games," Rachel added.

"Or Rachel and Calvin Klein clearance racks." Marco shot her a sidewise glance. She ignored him.

<Ah. Yes. As we say on the home world: "A test of will may lead to wisdom; a loss of will breeds but defeat.">

"Hey, I saw that same thing in a fortune cookie once."

"Where are Jake and Erek?" Rachel demanded.

<They'll be here in about five seconds,> I said. My job is to handle security for meetings. From my perch in the rafters I can look out through the open hayloft and watch the road and Cassie's house. And with red-tail ears I can hear just about anything approaching.

"Hey, everybody!" Jake said loudly. "Sorry we're late, but Erek has breaking news. Listen up!"

"As I told Jake," Erek started, "we know the Yeerks are ready to test the AMR. But they don't have a test subject," Erek continued.

<Why can't they use Visser Three?> I asked. <You know, get him to morph the nightmare alien beast-of-the-day, then turn the ray on him?>

"They could if he were volunteering. Which he isn't. Probably because there's a chance the

23

ray could prove fatal. And there's a possibility that a feedback effect could blow the weapon up."

Rachel brightened. "Well, that's a hopeful thought, at least."

"Man," Cassie said. She closed the bald eagle in its cage and came over to join the group. "So you're suggesting they want to test the AMR on one of us?"

Eric nodded. "The next time you make an appearance, I believe the Yeerks will do everything in their power to capture you. Or, failing that, at least fire the weapon at you."

"Well, then," Marco said, "we just won't get caught. We won't let them see us. Or hear us. Or smell us . . ."

"Or will we?" Jake interrupted.

Everyone turned to look at him. "Look, on the way over I started thinking."

"Had to happen sooner or later," Marco said in a loud whisper.

"Anyway, I was thinking, maybe that's exactly what we should do: Let the Yeerks capture one of us. Provide them with their test subject. Me, for instance. I let them take me prisoner. The rest of you follow secretly. They'll lead us straight to the AMR. Exactly where we want to go. In a position to destroy the weapon."

Marco spoke with disbelief. "I'm just going to

ask this once. Are you insane?? Jake, dude, think about it. Not that I should even be considering the details of a scheme as idiotic as this one, but what happens if we don't get there in time? If they drag you off and we can't trail you because we get held up by, oh, I don't know, a few dozen Hork-Bajir and a small army of Taxxons? The Yeerks get to use that AMR on you. And assuming it doesn't kill you — and that's assuming a lot — you know what they'll get when they forcibly demorph you? A human kid. Kiss our cover good-bye. Kiss us good-bye."

Rachel shook her head in disagreement. "Yeah, it's dangerous. But I say we do it. Jake just isn't the one to go. You're too important, Jake. We need you planning the attack on the AMR. So I volunteer."

Jake raised an arm to counter, but Ax broke in.

<Prince Jake, Rachel? If I may say so, I believe the only logical answer is for me to go. I am Andalite, after all. Should the AMR prove successful and the Yeerks are able to demorph me, they will get what they are expecting: an Andalite.>

"Makes sense," Marco said. "I mean, given that we're even talking this way, like we'd do it."

I watched Jake all this time. He was nodding. Like he bought what everyone was saying. But he was remaining quiet. So was Erek.

Jake had another idea in mind. He was just waiting for someone else to suggest it.

"You could die, Ax," Cassie emphasized. "Are you sure you want to do this?"

Ax spread-planted his hooves firmly, squared his shoulders, and looked us all in the eyes.

<I am sure.>

"We don't know where they're keeping the AMR," Jake said, not committing.

Now Marco was watching Jake. He'd seen the same reluctance I'd seen on Jake's face. The same holding back.

We were missing something. I knew that much. I just wasn't sure what it was. And then I knew.

<Guys. Wait a minute,> I interrupted.

"What is it?" Jake asked.

I swooped down from the rafter to the floor. Loose straw swirled in small eddies as I touched down. A ray of light from a crack in the barn wall bathed my feathers in yellow light. It was almost too much. Too theatrical. I half-expected angels to hover up out of the hayloft and break into song.

<It's me,> I said. <I'm the one who has to go.>

# CHAPTER 5

I saw the confirmation in Jake's eyes. And in the hologram that gave Erek eyes.

Marco clicked about a second later.

<Look, they turn the ray on Ax in morph, right?> I said. <If it works they get an Andalite. And they get proof the AMR works.>

Cassie nodded, reluctant. Rachel kept her eyes down. She was biting her lip. Angry, sad: the two emotions are very close together in Rachel.

<I'm the one,> I repeated. <The Yeerks don't know hawk is my true form. They'll think hawk is a morph. They capture me in morph, so they think, as a hawk. They turn the ray on me, nothing will happen. I mean, they won't get an An-

dalite or a human. They'll decide the ray doesn't work.>

There was a brief, thought-filled silence.

Then, slowly, all eyes turned toward me.

Cassie first, with that look of tender knowing she reserves for moments of significance. I could tell she was proud of me. And worried.

Rachel's eyes were different. Dark, almost stricken.

Marco sent an ironic bow in my direction. "You're right, Tobias. Don't you wish you weren't?"

Jake made a face I see too often. It's a look of disgust. Disgust with himself. He hadn't wanted to single me out, make me go on what might be a suicidal mission. He'd waited till I could volunteer.

<Tobias is correct,> Ax said. <But the mission could last longer than two hours. To play the part convincingly — to make the Yeerks think you're an Andalite in morph — you will have to "demorph" to Andalite at some point, Tobias. I believe you will need to acquire me.>

<Acquire you?>

<Yes, of course.>

Acquire Ax? None of us had ever morphed an Andalite before. What would it be like? I felt a sudden, overwhelming rush of anticipation. Mixed with anxiety. I chose not to share it.

<Yeah, I might have to.> I let it go at that.

"The trick now is to choose the best time and place," Jake said. "We have to act fast. But we want to be in control of the capture as much as possible."

"And it has to look credible," Cassie added. "I mean, the Yeerks have to believe it's a legitimate coup on their part. They can't suspect a setup."

"So, when?" Marco asked.

"I say tonight," Rachel answered. She still looked troubled. Her enthusiasm sounded forced.

"Tonight is the first night of The Sharing's three-day extravaganza with the new community center," Erek noted.

Marco rolled his eyes. "Yeah, we saw the ads on TV. Yeerk-a-Thon. They built the new community center and now they're going to broadcast the dedication. Full media coverage. A huge deal. They're obviously drawing members from other states, going more nationwide."

"We were planning on being there one of the nights anyway," Jake said. "To identify new 'full members' and learn more about the extent of The Sharing's influence."

"I can't go tonight, not on such short notice," Cassie said. "My parents will be back by evening. I can't just disappear."

"We can't pass up this chance to get close. I think we should risk it," Jake decided. "The

29

biggest night of the convention: awards cere-
mony. My brother's actually slated to get an
achievement award. I bowed out earlier when
Tom asked me to go. There's some big outdoor
banquet, with tents and music and games. I'll
tell him I changed my mind."

"Yeah, Jake should go as himself," Marco
said, snapping into his head-of-security mode.
"At an open-air function like that, you know
Yeerk security will be out to nab anything that
could be an Andalite in morph. The ants on the
buffet table, the flies on the hamburgers, the
birds in the trees. Jake's probably safest as a human, though not much help. If Erek's right, and
they're looking to capture us, it means they'll be
on the alert like never before."

"There's something else you need to know,"
Erek added. "We do not think the Yeerks built
this community center out of concern for the
community."

"I'm shocked," Marco said, then laughed.

"We only have a few hints. Some vague information. But we think there is some underground
construction there, probably a subterranean con-
nection to the Yeerk pool."

All eyes fixed on Erek.

"Oh, I like the sound of that," Marco replied
sarcastically. "Perfect. We can swing by the
Yeerk pool and do a little damage on our way to

30

save Tobias and blow up the AMR. Absolutely. Not a problem."

"Listen, everybody head home. Make contact with the parentals and meet back here early tonight if you can." There was energy in Jake's voice. "We have work to do. And, um, Tobias?"

<Yeah?>

"Get some rest. This isn't going to be a picnic for you."

# CHAPTER 6

Ax and I were busy with our own preparations that evening.

Ax climbed the steep rise of the hill near his scoop and I hitched a ride on a fading thermal. It was dusk. The sun was enormous on the horizon, about to disappear. Vibrant orange and purple warmed the forest. I landed on a low branch in a clearing on the hilltop.

<Tobias,> Ax said as he reached the clearing, <this is a special moment, is it not?>

<How do you mean?> I answered carefully.

<Well, you are . . .> Ax hesitated in an uncharacteristic way. <I mean, we are related, are we not? You are not Andalite, exactly, but you carry the Andalite heritage. I am glad you will

have that DNA in you from now on. It is a very unique genetic mixture.>

<Oh, we all know how much you think of your species, Ax,> I kidded.

<I do hold Andalites in very high regard. It is true. But it isn't an unthinking allegiance. I honestly admire my culture. There are things I would like to teach you, to share with you if you are interested.>

If I was interested! I wanted so much to stay cool. To make it seem like I could take it or leave it. But this was something, finally, that I really did have a right to. I was part Andalite, even if not genetically. God knew how. Or at least The Ellimist knew how. But I was. And it excited me.

<I'm ready anytime, Ax,> I managed to say.

He lifted me off the branch with gentle arms and set me on his shoulder. I squeezed as carefully as I could with my talons. I felt his muscles slacken as I acquired him.

I fluttered to the ground and focused. Morphing is always a crazy experience. You never know what body part will appear first. The way you transform is always a surprise.

The first thing I felt were my stalk eyes, growing out of my still-hawk head like two hyperactive worms. I heard the eyeballs form at the ends.

Paamp! Poomp!

Eyes that could see anywhere, everywhere, all

33

the time. Three-hundred sixty degrees of vision flooded my consciousness. Like a jolt. Because I could see most everything that could see me, I had control over my environment.

<Yaowww!> I gasped as I slowly rose off the ground. With one eye shifted to the back, I witnessed a huge, muscular rump grow out of my rusty tail feathers. And although I couldn't see them yet, I could feel four strong legs support me, responding to my growing bulk.

Muscles! Who would believe the easy strength. I stepped forward. A movement that took almost nothing out of me.

My tail! Unexpected. Yet an extension so natural I'd almost failed to notice how I carried it, erect and steadied at about shoulder level. The blade edge glistened in the sun's final rays. I was equipped for this world. For any world, really. A natural weapon. If I'd been in touch with my Andalite heritage before now, I could have sailed through elementary school bully-free. . . .

And then I recognized the Andalite mind.

Yes, it was all the things I'd imagined it would be. Confident. Alert. Poised for combat.

But there was another element that took me off guard. Something bubbling happily away beneath the rationality. Nothing giddy like a dolphin's playfulness. Something less simple.

Optimism. That was it. Intense optimism.

<Man! I had no idea.> I turned my head toward Ax. His eyes were smiling, the way they do.

<Keep in mind that you are experiencing instinct. The Andalite mind in its untrained state. Our culture teaches us to temper and control our optimism, to give equal value to realism. We have become, regrettably, a race of warriors. But that is in response to necessity. Down deeper, beneath that, I believe we are a peaceful species, in love with learning, not combat. But to learn — and to fight — you must be joyful. I think an ancient Andalite inscribed that on a *shormitor*.>

Ax whipped his tail blade through the air.

Fwapp!

<*Shormitor?*>

<Tail-blade carvings. Made by early Andalites. Mostly in the rocky outcroppings on the shores of the *Elupera*. We toured them once when I was much younger.>

<Ah.>

<In fact, it was on *shormitors* of the *Elupera* that I learned the early tail-fighting masters spent a lifetime trying to cultivate and listen to instinct. Trying to forget what culture had taught them. Let the innate defense mechanism kick in, as you humans say. You should have a natural advantage in this regard, Tobias,> Ax said as he

swung his tail in a figure eight, stopping just a centimeter short of the tree trunk. <That's not to say there aren't many maneuvers to be learned.>

I flexed the massive muscle that was my tail. I was tentative. I imitated the figure-eight exercise Ax was doing.

<I will teach you something,> Ax said, backing up. <A move I rely on frequently. The *torf*. You begin a common strike and then, millimeters before impact, twist your blade to the side, so that only the flat of the blade connects with the target. It won't do much to a Hork-Bajir, but it will knock a human unconscious. We will use this trunk as a target.>

Ax repeated the move in slow motion for me to see. But I wasn't paying complete attention. I could see in all directions at once. Front, back, left, right. At the same time!

<It is your turn.> Ax motioned to me.

I neared the tree, centered myself, and shifted my weight to my hind legs as Ax had.

<Now!> Ax yelled.

I let it rip. My tail hurtled toward the trunk.

FWAPP!

<Ahhh! Oh! Ouch! Ax?!>

<Yes, Tobias. You have impaled the tree with the tip of your blade. That is not the desired result.>

<Yeah, I sorta guessed that.>

I yanked and twisted. I couldn't free my blade.

<You struck with impressive velocity,> Ax observed. <That, at least, is admirable.>

<Yeah, great. You know you're a warrior when you take down a tree. And can't get your blade back.>

Ax grabbed my arms and leaned back. After a few seconds, <Ahhh!> Ax pulled so hard that when my tail came free, I rammed into him and sent us both tumbling down.

<Ahhhhhh!>

We landed in a heap. Eight legs tangled.

<I should have let you familiarize yourself with the Andalite body before suggesting tail-blade practice. We will refresh ourselves with a drink, and perform the evening ritual.>

We walked over to a nearby stream. Ax stuck a hoof in. So did I. I waited to see what I should do next. It was so pleasant, this cool, gurgling brook. So refreshing. So satisfying.

<Ax, this is very, very cool.>

Wait. What? I was drinking! I looked at my hoof. It looked normal. But the thirst in my . . . in my legs was being quenched. It was amazing. It was also a little creepy.

The very last glimmer of color was disappearing from the sky, absorbed by the mysterious indigo of night.

&lt;Look to the last bit of orange,&gt; Ax said. &lt;That's how the ritual begins.&gt;

I stopped drinking and turned all eyes on the stripe of color.

&lt;From the rising of the sun to the setting, to its rising again,&gt; Ax said, &lt;we place what is hard to endure with what is sweet to remember, and find peace.&gt;

He stopped.

&lt;That's it?&gt;

&lt;That is it.&gt;

&lt;I like it.&gt;

&lt;Me too.&gt;

# CHAPTER 7

**S**aturday night. The grandest night of The Sharing's giant publicity gala.

I cruised over town, skimming above the neon McDonald's signs and telephone poles and car headlights, toward the new community center.

Faint at first, then more definite, came sounds from the celebration. Voices filtered through night air. Jaunty strains of a jazz band. Shrieks and giggles from the younger members. And above it all — over the acoustic wash that grew more insistent the nearer I got — boomed a deep, formal voice.

"Ladies and gentlemen, boys and girls. Good evening . . ."

Tall, white tents reached up into my airspace.

Spotlights crisscrossed the sky. Stage lights illuminated the podium and the blue-suited master of ceremonies below. Round, white-clothed tables dotted the grass.

<Jake, Ax, I'm here,> I called down into the crowd. As long as I stayed clear of the spotlights, I knew I could fly fairly low without being seen. Even so, I kept a sharp eye on the human-Controller security guards who lined the perimeter.

I caught sight of Jake. In a dress shirt and tie, seated at a banquet table next to Tom, his dad, and his mom.

<You look extremely uncomfortable,> I said in thought-speak.

He couldn't answer me. But he rolled his eyes in agreement, then turned his head to the right and nodded toward the buffet table.

"That's three!" somebody exclaimed.

"Is he getting another one?"

The shouts were coming from the end, where an elderly man stood next to a cotton candy cart, surrounded by children.

"Son, I just don't think it's safe to give you any more. Where are your parents?"

I circled around, trying to see what Jake wanted me to notice. Trying to stay up, out of the lights.

There was Ax, in human morph. Wisps of pink

cotton candy streaked his hair, hung from his chin like a ghostly beard, and blew from his fingers as he forced his way to the front of the line.

I laughed. Ax with a human mouth is dangerous. Andalites have only a vestigial sense of taste. Nothing like the explosive sensory overload from the human mouth.

I looked back at Jake. He was shaking his head slightly, like an exasperated, but amused, parent.

<Ax-man! It's Tobias. You've got to get control of your morph. Right now. You can't make a scene.>

<Tobias?> Ax wondered in thought-speak. <Oh, Tobias! This cloud candy is superb. It is otherworldly. The way it melts on the tongue. It has mass, yet it is weightless . . .>

<Oh, boy. Ax, where are the others? You're supposed to be helping me guide them. They're in fly morph, don't forget. They can smell dog poop and see about six inches, and that's it.>

"Friends . . ." the man at the podium continued. "Three words encapsulate The Sharing's appeal: Opportunity. Involvement. Dedication. Change. Hmm, that's four." There was a slight pause and feedback hum as he thought that one over. "But then, that's just like The Sharing, isn't it? Exceeding expectations." The crowd cheered approval. "Tonight we honor members who embody these words. Who, with their achievement, keep our organization running on course . . ."

<Help! Help!> Marco sputtered. Then added a violent, <Ax!>

<Marco?> I cried. <Marco, you in fly morph?>

<Chocolate-covered, man. I'm in the chocolate fondue and they've turned up the heat! Buffet table! Buffet table! I can't get out!>

<Fondue?> Ax asked.

<A warm pot of chocolate. Liquid. Brown.> I couldn't think of how to describe it. From fifty feet up I scanned the buffet table. Marco was black against dark brown. I could barely see him at this distance.

<Marco, what exactly are you doing in the fondue?> Rachel asked.

<Exactly? Well . . . I wanted to see if it would still taste good sucked up through a fly mouth. You gonna help me or do you just want to bust me?>

<Let him get eaten,> Rachel advised.

Ax moved toward the chocolate fondue. A fly buzzed out of his cotton candy beard. This fly was more easily visible: black against pink.

<Rachel? Is that you?> I called down.

<Could be, how would I know what fly you're looking at? I was just in the middle of this big cloud, sticky and sweet and . . . Where's Cassie?

Where's Ax? Man! Five minutes in and we're all messed up.>

<I'm fine,> Cassie said. <At least, I think I am.>

<Okay, that is you, Rachel, just follow the cotton candy. It's Ax. The sticky cloud.>

<Is there some reason you think I'm not fine?> Cassie pressed, anxious now.

<Cotton candy?> Rachel said. <Huh? What is he doing eating cotton . . . Oh, never mind.>

"This year's highest honor goes to a young man who moved swiftly to the top of our ranks," the emcee intoned. "A devoted member of our community." Applause thundered through the crowd. Tom rose from his chair and accepted a plaque.

<What do you see? What's the matter?> Cassie demanded.

<Nothing, Cassie. Tom's getting his award,> I reported. <Ax-man. Careful grabbing Marco. Cassie? Are you near Jake?>

Naturally Jake heard all this, since we'd included him in our thought-speak. He was fidgeting. Nervous. Looking like he was about to jump out of his chair and run for the fondue. Or maybe just for the exit.

Then I saw Jake's eyes roll up toward the sky in what could only be an expression of "Why me?" I glanced back at Ax to see what had upset Jake. The Andalite was wearing a pink, cotton candy beard and had his hand immersed in the chocolate fondue. The chocolate was up to his wrist.

He pulled his hand out, held it up in front of his face like he'd just discovered it was made out of gold, then began licking his fingers.

# CHAPTER 8

<Ax! Ax! You'll eat Marco!>

<He will?> Marco shrilled. <What do you mean, he'll eat me?>

Disgusted bystanders backed away from the dessert area, pointing.

<I'm on something! I'm moving. Hey! I'm . . . I'm . . . I'm dripping!>

Light! Blinding light! A searchlight beam had swung wildly. I flared my tail, cranked my wings, flew out of the light.

Had I been seen? The Yeerks had seen a red-tailed hawk. Way too many times, in all the wrong places. Had they seen me now?

<I've dripped!> Marco yelled. <I . . . Okay, I'm off Ax's hands. I'm back on the surface of the

45

chocolate. Near the edge. Don't eat me! I'm serious: Do not eat me!>

<Use a strawberry. Ax! Use a strawberry!>

Ax, Rachel, Cassie, and Marco all said, <What?>

<It's what you dip in the fondue,> I yelled. <Ax, grab a strawberry! Use it to dip him out.>

<Dip the dip,> Rachel added, not at all helpfully.

Ax grabbed a strawberry, and with the concentration of a brain surgeon, lifted Marco from the steaming pot.

<Okay, Ax, listen very carefully,> Marco hissed. <Do not eat the strawberry. I repeat: Do not —>

<Guys,> I cut in. <Visser Three just arrived. In human morph, of course.>

There was no mistaking him. The tall, distinguished-looking man who agilely descended the stairs from back of the stage to congratulate Tom's family. In the most superficial of ways, I suppose he could pass for your average, benign suit. But if you actually looked at him, you sensed that incredible coldness. Emptiness. The dark evil that destroys life like a hand closing strong fingers around your throat.

Standing just back from the Visser were four guys who could only be security. They looked like the kind of guys you'd see with a Mafia don.

Visser Three worked the main table like a politician. He stopped by Jake's family. He shook hands all around. Patted Tom on the shoulder. Weird thing was, even Tom seemed to squirm a little.

<So, what's happening? I'm getting bored,> Rachel demanded.

A fly buzzed past the Visser's ear. Slap!

<Cassie! Was that you?!> I yelled.

Jake had gone pale. He was staring, staring as the Visser pulled his hand away from his own face and examined his palm.

<I'm okay,> Cassie said. <Missed me. Fly reflexes. Very cool. It was close, though.>

"A fly!" the Visser said. "A fly!" he snapped to his guards. The four human-Controllers bounded forward.

I didn't see Cassie. I was torn. Should I go lower? Risk being noticed? Then I caught sight of a fly again.

Cassie circled Jake and landed on his forehead. <Where am I? I'm not sure.>

Visser Three jumped forward.

"Such filthy insects. Allow me to . . ." He swung at Jake. Jake's hand shot up. He grabbed the Visser's wrist in his fist.

For a long few seconds the two of them glared at each other. Visser Three, leader of the Yeerk forces on Earth. And Jake, his unrecognized foe.

47

<Cassie? MOVE!> I yelled.

She flew. I lost her again.

Jake released the Visser's hand. Jake smiled. The Visser smiled. Or at least they formed their mouths into smiles.

<Cassie? Are you clear?>

<Yeah. I think I'm in Jake's shirt pocket.> Then she laughed. <The Visser just told Jake he hoped he didn't scare him. Jake said, "I don't scare easy.">

<That's our boy,> I said.

Visser Three moved on down the table. Everyone breathed. Jake leaned over to say something to his parents. Then he got up.

He walked straight through the buffet line, found Ax, and grabbed him by the arm, not at all gently.

A second later Ax was talking to us all. <Prince Jake says "Enough messing around, let's do what we came here to do.">

What we had come here to do was turn me over to the Yeerks.

Personally, I wouldn't have minded some more messing around.

# CHAPTER 9

Jake and Ax parted ways. Jake went around the back of the community center building. Back away from the lights. He tried two of the doors. Both locked.

He stepped away into the darkness and reappeared a moment later carrying a cinder block. Part of the leftover debris of construction.

He stood there, waiting. I flew above, waiting. He didn't look up. He knew I was there.

<All clear, Jake,> I said.

He nodded. Then he swung the cinder block into a low window. The tinkling of glass was swallowed up in the booming sound of the emcee's voice announcing the next honoree.

Jake stepped away quickly.

I took aim on the shattered glass. Plenty of room for me, if I folded my wings. More than enough room for the others, once they found their way there.

Down I flew, down through the cool, dark air, focusing on the glittering outline. Down through reaching shards of glass that could slice me open, end to end.

But of course I'm more accurate than that. I can hit a mouse on the run through tall grass. Flying through a hole in a window is really nothing special.

Zoom! Through! I flared my wings and tail, killed my speed, then resumed level flight.

Fluorescent lights illuminated a wide hallway with tall cinder block walls. I smelled new construction — fresh paint, drywall dust. And chlorine, coming from the Olympic-size indoor pool I saw through a wall of glass.

It suddenly struck me just what level of cash flow The Sharing controls. Serious cash. Not the kind of money you make selling Furbies on the black market.

I zoomed past playrooms. Lego tables, costumes, board games. A large meeting room with a giant table. Big, comfy office chairs. The rooms were empty. Everyone was celebrating the dedication outdoors.

It's hard flying indoors. No head wind, no tailwind, no thermals. Nothing but flat, dead air. And very little room to maneuver, hemmed in above, below, and on both sides.

But at the same time, it's exhilarating. A roller coaster for birds. One wrong move and you crumple a wing. Humans think it's scary to be up high, but not for a bird. For a bird altitude is safety.

I turned a corner and practically ran into Ax. I landed on his back, enjoying the respite.

<Hey, shouldn't you be in some slightly less provocative morph?> I asked him.

<Possibly. But I felt a strong, fast tail might prove useful.>

<Ax-man, we're not here to win. We're here to let me be captured.>

<True. And yet there is no reason why I cannot do some damage. Merely by way of adding authenticity and realism.>

I was touched. He was worried about me.

Ahead was a set of stairs leading down to the basement level. They were roped off, marked with a hastily written sign: UNDER CONSTRUCTION. KEEP OUT.

<This looks promising,> Ax murmured.

<This looks like trouble,> I muttered.

<As you pointed out: We are here in search of trouble.>

He walked down the stairs with a catlike

51

tread. Or with a tread as close to catlike as you can manage while crunching construction debris under hoof.

The basement was dim and filled with building materials. Piles of floor tile in one corner. A stack of plywood sheathing against the wall. A contractor's table saw. Plastic tarps.

<Maybe it really is just construction,> I said. <Nobody's down here. If there were access to the Yeerk pool, wouldn't there be people coming and going? Not to mention elaborate security.>

Before the words were out of my mouth, I realized I'd spoken too soon. Behind the stairs, shielded by a temporary partition, flickered blue-green light. Computer screens. An entire wall of them! Flashing camera images from the celebration outside. The stage. The food tent. The playground. The bandstand. Over the door hung another makeshift sign: EVENT SECURITY.

One man sat with his back to us, watching the screens. Mesmerized by the flickering images.

Without warning came the echo of hard heels pounding the concrete floor. Rapid, metered steps. Approaching.

Next to the surveillance room was another door. Ax moved quickly toward it. He pushed on it. Just as I noticed the arrow taped to the wall above. BREAK ROOM, the arrow read.

The door opened. And there, directly in front of us, were four Hork-Bajir. Seated around a card table. Elbow blades hanging casually off the chairs. Tails slung back across the floor. Each held a hand of cards tightly in his claws. A single, unshaded lightbulb dangled from the ceiling.

<Let's try a different door.>

Ax backed out instantly. The Hork-Bajir hadn't noticed us.

I could feel the vibrations of Ax's hearts hammering. My own heart was a machine gun.

The footsteps were now just yards away.

No choice. Back, into the security room. Hope the guard on duty there was still watching his screens. Hope we didn't make a sound.

Ax spun, leaped; I slipped my hold, opened my wings, caught just enough air to keep from hitting the floor and followed Ax as he dived awkwardly beneath a steel table.

Too much noise! The guard had to hear us. Had to!

But no. Nothing. He still watched his screens. The enemy was out there, out somewhere in camera range. Not right here, in the same room.

The footsteps from the hallway followed us. Stopped. Four black boots, inches away. One pair was crusted with dried mud.

"See anything?" Muddy Boots asked the TV man.

53

"Nah. Thought I saw some kid heading round the back. Then I lost him."

An acknowledging grunt from Clean Boots.

I wasn't too worried these guys would get us. Ax's tail was cocked and ready. The table would go flying and these two would be counting in base five before they could draw their weapons.

But that would cause an uproar. The Hork-Bajir would come running, and it wasn't time for me to be captured. Not yet. Not till we knew where the secret entrance was.

Funny I should think that particular thing. The next words out of the guard's mouth were, "Just left the entrance. Passed off my shift to Lacsar-Four-Fifty-Four."

I was further forward than Ax. I could, by shifting ever so slightly, see the men. Two guys who looked like regular security guards. Except for the Dracon beams holstered in their belts.

"Any animals?" the TV man asked, never glancing away from the screens. He wasn't mesmerized by the screens, I realized. He'd been ordered not to look away. On pain of death.

"We kicked a few dogs. Sprayed some bugs. Waste of time, you can't keep every possible animal morph out of an open-air celebration. Could have told Visser Three that."

"Yeah, you could have," his partner, Clean

Boots, said dryly. "And about three seconds later you'd be begging for your life."

A rueful laugh. "Got that right. Anyway, I do have to see the sub-visser about . . . Ouch!"

"What is it?"

"Something stuck in my shoe . . ." He knelt down to unlace it. His profile suddenly so close we could see the stubble on his chin. The pores on his nose. There was no way! No way he wouldn't notice us!

"Darn wood chips drive me crazy! Sharp like pins! I hate that lousy entrance shift," he muttered. "Tromping around like I'm some human eight-year-old."

The guard stood up, slipped off the shoe, and knocked it against the table leg, showering Ax with topsoil. And a wood chip. I breathed. Ax breathed.

They walked on. Past us and toward the wall of cameras, where a man sat, his back to us, monitoring the pictures.

"Hello, Chief," they addressed him. "Come to give our reports."

<Ax,> I said tersely. <Look at the camera images.>

He turned.

Of the fifty or so screens, nearly half pictured the same spot. All from different angles, so it wasn't immediately obvious. But the more I focused the more I realized . . .

<Wood chips.>

<It appears to be a sort of skeletal construction, of some sort. Metal components as well as wood. Its purpose is not immediately apparent.>

<It's a playground, Ax-man. Swing set. Jungle gym. And a tunnel.>

# CHAPTER 10

It took an hour for Ax and me to extricate ourselves and round up the others.

The big Yeerk-a-Thon was winding up. They were making closing speeches. The six of us were above and around the playground. While we'd watched, three people had crawled in through the kiddie tunnel. None had crawled out the far side.

It was a pretty elaborate structure, really. Two stories. Built of large posts maybe half the height of telephone poles. With a mesh net for climbing, a fireman's pole, a wide metal slide. And intricate covered catwalks. Far cooler than anything I'd ever played on.

The playground itself was surrounded on two

sides by trees, with an open playing field at the far end, and the community center wall defining the left side.

We'd spotted guards atop the community center, guards in the woods, guards pretending to sit idly on the bleachers behind the batting cage.

A least eight human-Controllers were watching the playground. A lot of security for a jungle gym at night.

A person was approaching, a man, feet crunching across the wood chips.

<It's Tasset,> Jake said. He was in owl morph, with eyes that saw through the night like it was noon on a cloudless day. <From the sporting goods store,> Jake whispered. <One of our known Controllers. ID'd him at the Yeerk pool.>

<Okay, we'll follow him in,> Cassie said. <Just tell us which way.>

<Yeah, 'cause, see, we're blind down here.>

Marco, Cassie, and Rachel had stayed in fly morph. They would try and enter the tunnel. And come back out again.

Ax was out of camera range behind some trees. He was standing between two guards, not twenty feet from either of them. Needless to say, he was standing very still.

<You should see a row of square lights,> Jake

directed. His owl morph was better for this kind of night work. I could see the flies. Jake could SEE them. <Those are the windows of the community center. Keep those on your left. Okay, now I've lost one of you. Never mind, got you back. Close up. Stay together. Drift a little to the right. Now just hover there.>

I landed soundlessly on one of the jungle gym poles and perched still as a statue. I had seen the camera angles and knew where to be to stay out of view.

Tasset stooped and disappeared under the slide.

<I see him,> said Cassie. <He's blue and green and there are about ninety pictures of him, but I definitely see him.>

Cassie and Marco flew behind Tasset. The cameras would never pick them up. But there might be other dangers. There were always other dangers.

<Red lights, I think,> Marco called. <I think maybe he popped open a hidden panel. Up under the slide. Possibly red light. Who can tell? You all know what fly vision is like.>

I felt the featherlight touch of Rachel landing on my back and nestling down under the feathers.

I heard a faint cascade of beeps coming from below my perch.

*Dee-deep.*

*Dee-dee-dee-dee.*

Tasset moved out from under the slide and crouched to enter the adjoining concrete tunnel.

<Come into my lair!> Marco joked in a Dracula voice. <Moooah-ha-ha-ha!>

The tunnel was large, like one of those big concrete sewer pipes. You couldn't quite stand up in it, but you didn't have to crawl, either.

Tasset was about to go in when two other Controllers poked their heads out of the tunnel. He backed up to let them pass. Which they did. Silently.

<Now we've got traffic,> Jake said.

Ax spoke up for the first time. <Prince Jake, I see additional humans approaching. I may have to withdraw.>

<Do what you have to do, but stay close for the big finale. You may need to remove one or more of the guards,> Jake said tersely. <Marco? Where are you and Cassie? You're out of my line of sight.>

<We are right behind this guy's big butt,> Marco said. <And we see light at the end of the tunnel.>

<Good grief,> Rachel muttered. <This is so not the time for your feeble attempts at being funny.>

Rachel always teases Marco. That was nothing new. But there was a deeper note of stress in her thought-speak voice.

<He's not kidding,> Cassie said, surprised. <There's an intense light. Although I'd say it's more toward the middle than the end. Looks like another control panel. Yeah. There! I'm landing on it! I think Tasset's punching in a code word, but . . . Yah! Whoa. He just punched whatever number I was sitting on.>

I heard a sound like a pneumatic pump, or a seal being broken, then a rush of air.

Psssst.

Woooooosh!

<Ahhhhhh!>

<Yeeeeooooow!>

Two flies shot out the near end of the green tunnel, back to where they'd started.

<Yee-hah!> Marco exulted.

<There's something in there, all right,> Cassie said.

<With a serious pressure diff going. That was one heck of a ride!>

<Okay, back out,> Jake ordered. <Cassie? Marco? You guys are done. Ax? Are you set?>

I heard a faint "Fwapp!" from the trees. Followed by a crumpling sound. A human would not have heard either noise.

<Yes, Prince Jake. I am in place. There is one less guard.>

61

<Okay, me and Cassie wish you all luck, and we are motoring on outta here,> Marco said. Then he laughed. <The Yeerks have no respect for our intelligence, do they? Like we wouldn't know this was a trap? Like we'd think a sewer pipe in a playground was a sensible entrance for the Yeerk pool?>

<A setup,> Rachel said. <Bait. Maybe they figured that even if we sensed a trap we couldn't resist.>

<Yeah, and it turns out they were right,> Cassie said darkly.

<But there are two levels of security, over and above the guards,> I pointed out. <That seems meticulous, doesn't it? Code-activated panels under the slide and in the tunnel? If they want us in, why make it complicated? Not the easiest thing to infiltrate.>

<Unless we were to forget stealth,> Rachel remarked, with growing excitement in her tone, <and go with the old standbys.>

<What are those?>

<Force and surprise,> she said. Then she laughed self-consciously.

Marco said, <You know, Rachel, when you're in fly morph, talking ruthlessly about guerrilla warfare, and force and surprise and all, I just find it so exciting, and yet disturbing. You know? Like a Britney Spears video with tanks.>

<Well, okay, it's a trap,> I said. <A trap is what we came for. Let's just get this over with.>

Nobody said anything. Everyone knew that's what needed to happen. We'd discussed it. Planned it. It was just that none of us had ever willingly surrendered before.

Another Controller walked out of the community center and started across the wood chips, toward the slide.

<Okay, Tobias. You ready?> Jake asked.

<Can't say I'm looking forward to it,> I said. <But yeah.>

<Rachel?>

<Me? Who do you think you're talking to?> She feigned surprise at his question. <Bring on the ambush!>

But I heard the struggle in her voice. She was masking concern. Why? Rachel never worried. At least not about herself.

<Tobias?> she said softly in private thought-speak.

<What is it? Do you want out?>

<No, of course not. It's not that.> She paused. <Listen. Um. You take care of yourself. I mean . . . be careful. Okay? Whatever happens? If it comes down to it, save yourself and forget the stupid mission.>

I smiled inwardly. She was concerned about me. If I had been human . . . looking into

Rachel's eyes, feeling her next to me, I might have . . . But she was a fly on my hawk body. Which was good. I could keep my cool. A hawk's feelings aren't exactly visible to others.

<I will,> I said simply. Then added, <I have a lot to lose.>

# CHAPTER 11

<Everyone out. Everyone but Tobias and Rachel,> Jake ordered. <Ax? Be ready. I'm going for the lights.>

An owl, silent as a ghost, flew overhead, swooping toward the community center building.

The Controller approached, ducked under the slide.

I heard the flickering LEDs.

*Dee-deep. Dee-dee-dee-dee.*

<Yeah, we're in it dee-deep, all right,> Rachel muttered.

The faint electronic chime met my ear just as a ripping gust of wind rose up and whistled through the jungle gym.

Sheeeewooooo.

A cold wind that ruffled my feathers and sent a chill down my spine. I lifted off. Powered my wings to gain altitude. A rope banged a hollow note on the metal flagpole. The leaves on the trees rustled and swished with the air. And the emcee's voice from back at The Sharing's celebration rang out above it all.

"Pride in our work . . . dedication to the task at hand . . . never, never ceasing. We will reach our goal."

Thunderous applause.

The Controller disappeared from view, into the tunnel.

<Jake! Ax! Now!> I yelled.

Ax erupted from hiding, galloping madly toward the tunnel.

I spilled air from my wings and fell into a dive, gaining speed every instant.

<Hang on!> I yelled to Rachel.

We shot toward the earth. Aimed for the tunnel.

"Andalites!" a guard cried, startled.

Ax shot into the tunnel.

I veered a violent right, just a few feet from the playground. Into the tunnel. Insane! Too fast! No way to control my speed!

Wings and tail straining, straining, catching all the air I could catch, straining to absorb the energy of my own momentum.

A circle of white light. The silhouette of a man. An Andalite, bent low, tail whipping.

FWAPP!

The Controller dropped.

Man, Andalite, a circle of light, beeping panel, wings flapping, the grainy curved walls of the tunnel, all in millisecond flashes.

<Ax! Go! GO!>

He shot away just as I blew into the tunnel, banked into a turn that nearly ripped the ligaments out of my wings, and shot through into the circle of light.

From outside a voice roared, almost hysterical. "Andalites!"

<Now, Prince Jake!> Ax cried.

Outside the lights of the playground were snapping on. Outside Ax, now clearly illuminated, was running for his life, pursued by all the guards.

That was the plan. Ax risking his life for no purpose but to make it all look real, to make it all seem as if I'd been trapped in the midst of a genuine attack.

Ax might die. For the sake of realistic drama.

The door slid closed.

Psssst. Click. I could feel it seal tightly shut.

Darkness. My eyes saw nothing. But I heard . . .

"Ahhhgggg-ggghhhha. Ahhhgggg-ggghhhha."

My heart skipped a beat. I knew that sound. The throaty, heavy breathing of Yeerk-infested Hork-Bajir. Pumped up. Ready for action.

<Are we in?> Rachel called.

<We're in all right,> I whispered. <And we're not alone.>

# CHAPTER 12

Lights on!

Massive, spiky shapes. A wall of seething Hork-Bajir. Three dozen, maybe more. Waiting for me in the brightened passageway.

And a girl. A human. For a millisecond I thought . . . No, no, of course it wasn't Rachel. This girl was a couple of years older. Tall, thin, blond. Sleek chinos, leather loafers. A knit top even Rachel would admire.

Preppy.

Supermodel.

Yeerk.

I was speechless.

"Only one of you? And in bird morph?" she

69

sneered. "Oh, well," she continued confidently. "With one in hand, we'll soon catch the others."

Chapman cleared his throat. I hadn't even noticed him, standing there right next to her.

"A bird in the hand is worth two in the bush," he offered, smirking.

"Shut up, Chapman," the girl said calmly. "You sound like some pun-spouting villain from a Batman movie."

"Yes, ma'am. Excuse me, ma'am. I mean, sub-visser."

Sub-visser?

She stared at me like she could see right into my mind. Like she knew who I was, what I was. And wanted to hurt me because of it. I swallowed hard.

<Tobias, what's going on? Why aren't we moving?> Rachel was all energy. <Put up a fight! Let 'em know you don't want to be here. Come on, play the part.>

Right! She was right.

I let out a screeching cry. More for effect than for anything else. Hoping to scare them. They shuffled a bit as I flapped up. And then, airborne, I lunged at the nearest monstrous mass.

"Galaash! Ahhh!"

My outstretched talons gouged his eyes. Wrist blades slashed the air around me.

The blade sliced an inch off my tail. I couldn't

steer. I struggled to compensate with wing angle, to circle back and strike again.

Whaack! Wummph!

<Ahhh!> Something hard hit my head. The sub-visser's arm!

<What!> Rachel yelled.

I crumpled to the floor. Facedown in a heap. <We're down. I . . .> I tried to shake off the impact and raised my head from the stone. There was the sub-visser, standing over me. Her right arm gleaming a pearly, plastic white. Artificial! She'd struck me with an artificial arm.

"Didn't think we'd be waiting for you, did you, Andalite?" she said coldly. "Well, here we are. Surprised? I hope so. I love surprises, don't you?"

Chapman laughed appreciatively.

"Oh, did I forget to introduce myself?" She brought her hand to her cheek in a motion of mock surprise. "So sorry. I'm Sub-Visser Fifty-one. Second-in-command to Visser Three in this part of space. Call me Taylor."

"Her host name," Chapman explained.

"Shut *up,* Chapman!" she snarled and stamped her foot like any spoiled kid.

It was a bizarre performance. The usually glowering vice principal was fawning over a teenager from the pages of a J. Crew catalog.

"Nothing to say? Speechless?" Taylor taunted

71

me. "Come on, I've always wanted to talk to an Andalite. Trade a little banter with the high-and-mighty self-appointed lords of the galaxy. Do you think by staying silent I'll somehow be convinced you're an actual bird?"

She laughed. "No, no, friend Andalite. We've seen the red-tailed hawk before, haven't we? I said, haven't we, Chapman?"

"Yes, Sub-visser!"

<I have nothing to say. I am a prisoner of war.>

"Oh, good, it does speak," Taylor said and clapped her hands.

I knew I had to "demorph" to Andalite. Act my part. Make this ruse complete. There was no logical reason for me to stay in morph.

I focused my mind on a happier time, just hours earlier. I pictured Ax. I became Ax.

This time the tail came first. I felt it push out of my feathers and begin to grow, thick and wide, into its natural arc. Felt the blade emerging at the end. How I must have looked! A blue-tailed hawk.

The nearest Hork-Bajir started, ready to grab me where I lay. Taylor motioned them to hold. And leveled her artificial arm. Straight at me.

From the palm of her hand came a hissing noise, louder and louder, until . . .

*Shooopooof!*

From her hand exploded a spray of white, blinding particulates.

<Ahhh!> I cried. Stinging pain that seemed to coat my body.

<Ohhh!> Rachel felt it too.

Chapman and the Hork-Bajir tried to back away. Too late. The Hork-Bajir clawed at their own eyes. Chapman writhed, as if he was crawling with ants.

"What the —" he yelled, then fell silent.

Taylor smirked, unaffected.

Then, slowly, the pain passed and I felt . . . nothing. No feeling at all! My mind raced, but my body wouldn't respond. I fell back to the floor with a thud. Unable to move. Frozen in mid-morph. Paralyzed!

<What's going on?> Rachel cried. <I can't feel my legs. Or my wings. I can't move!>

<She shot us with a gas or something. She got Chapman, too. And a half-dozen Hork-Bajir.> They were falling to the ground like giant dominoes.

Thud. Thumpf.

Taylor's lips formed a broad, sinister grin.

"Surprise!" She laughed to herself, standing tall. Unfazed by the gas. "So sorry for you all. Looks like I'm the only one who remembered to take the antidote in advance. Oh, wait. Did I forget to tell you all?" Her laughter stopped abruptly. "Gather up these fools," she ordered, motioning to the remaining Hork-Bajir.

Then she walked over to where I lay and smiled again, eyes aglow with self-satisfaction.

And she called out, loudly enough so her henchmen could hear: "And pick up the Andalite filth, too. We have a special place all picked out for him."

Strong arms hoisted me off the floor by my Andalite tail. I was powerless to resist. Or even move a muscle.

<Tobias!> Rachel screamed with frustration. <I'm losing my grip! I can't hold on!>

I felt a stab of cold terror. No. No, if Rachel and I were separated . . . No one to bring word of the Anti-Morphing Ray's location to Jake. No one to bring rescue.

And Rachel? Left here, unseen, a fly? Paralyzed in morph? My God, she might never . . .

<Rachel! Try to demorph! Now! Do it!>

<I can't, they'd see me.>

<You want to be trapped as a fly? Forget the mission! Rachel!>

<Tobias! I'm slipping off your feathers! I'm falling!> It sounded like she was starting to cry.

Not a sound I'd ever expected to hear.

Minutes into the mission, and we were finished. Trapped. No way out. No help waiting.

A heavy metal door clanged shut. I was in a

dark corridor. Another Hork-Bajir held up a metal box, and the first one crammed me into it and sealed the opening shut, blacking out any hint of light.

<Rachel! Rachel!>

Bumps and jolts as the Hork-Bajir knocked the box against his leg with each step.

<Rachel! Rachel! Demorph! If you can, oh God, demorph!>

No answer. Silence in my head.

I was alone.

# CHAPTER 13

The darkness was complete.

Total.

And I heard nothing. No sound save my own irregular breathing.

Sensation started to return and I realized I'd been stuffed into a box half my size. A straitjacket that pinned my wings against my body. Jammed the vestigial Andalite tail up into my neck.

The hawk in me tensed every muscle. No room! In a panic, it pressed against the walls of the seamless steel box. Terrified. Confined. I fought to control the bird. But I was losing the struggle. The human me was frightened, too.

Rachel! Oh, Rachel. Could she escape this underground network? Somehow survive?

She would. Sure she would. She had to. She was Rachel, after all. Rachel!

Where was she? All I could think of was a paralyzed fly, helpless and vulnerable on the floor. Someone would step on her. She wouldn't be able to get out of the way, and someone would kill her.

Better than the alternative. Life as a fly. Trapped, like me. But so not like me. I could see, soar . . .

And the plan? Rachel was supposed to have seen where they took me, then lead the others in. First prove the Anti-Morphing Ray didn't work, then, in the rescue, destroy the thing for good measure.

It was crazy! Inconceivable arrogance on our parts. We had underestimated our foe. A fatal error. Fatal.

The hawk brain, the animal part that still, even now, lived apart from me, untouched by human reason, began a low, defeated moan. A death moan.

So hot in the box. Like an oven. Warmer, and warmer still. How much more oxygen could there be? Were they trying to suffocate me? Was that it?

Interminable!

The only external input were the wobbles and bobs as the holder of the box hit me against his leg. The ride continued.

No space to morph or demorph.

<I'll be trapped. As a horrific, half-morphed creature,> I pronounced slowly. <That will be my fate. I bet Andalites don't even have a word for that tragedy.>

That's it. Keep talking, Tobias. Keep talking. Stay sane. Hold on. Don't think . . .

Zeeewooozeeewooo.

All six walls of the box began to buzz. Vibrate. And then: Poosh!

Like a camera flash, steel walls vaporized. Dazzling light flooded my eyes. Blinded me. Rods and cones shot to hell. I saw nothing but white.

I blinked a few times. Then, no. No, my eyes were adjusting.

I was in another box. But a completely different kind. A cube of glass. Larger. Maybe four feet square. Big enough for me to move about. Brightly illuminated, with several spotlights directed at me. I demorphed immediately. Back to hawk.

I blinked again. And as I rose to my feet, I realized I was suspended. The cube hung in the center of a much larger room. I strained to look beyond the glass. Through the glare from the lights to the dimness beyond.

"There's no way out." It was Taylor's voice. Sub-Visser Fifty-one. Cold and casual. "There's no point in looking around."

She sat alone at a long table near the door of the large, gloomy, windowless room. To her right and left, armed Hork-Bajir, standing at attention. Above, a network of steel beams and conduits and a daunting maze of wire.

"You may as well demorph and make yourself comfortable while we wait," she continued.

*Nice try,* I thought. *Demorph and make myself comfortable. Yeah, right! Wouldn't she just love an Andalite to infest. That would get her noticed by the Visser. Why don't I plunge my head in the sludgy Yeerk pool while I'm at it?*

"No?" she prodded, mocking. "Don't want to demorph? Worried about that whole Yeerk-in-the-head thing? That's okay, my little Andalite birdie. You stay just the way you are. For now."

I looked again at the glass walls of my cube. Smooth and thick. Flawless. Featureless, except for one small, inset panel. In the panel were three circles. Three discs like oversized elevator buttons. They were colored. One red, one blue, one black.

"Ah, I see you've noticed the control device. There's a little experiment to be carried out as soon as Visser Three arrives," she said knowingly. "This device is state of the art, Andalite. The very latest in Yeerk technology."

A little experiment? Control device? The Anti-Morphing Ray. That had to be it. Right?

79

I reached forward with my beak to touch the panel.

Scheewack! Kewwwack! Force-field static crackled and hissed. An electric jolt grabbed my beak and sent a shock through my body. From wings to tail and back again. I collapsed, stunned, to the floor.

"Ouchie," Taylor said.

# CHAPTER 14

There was a loud banging on the door. Two Hork-Bajir scurried to open it, knocking into each other on the way. A clatter of arm blades as they struggled to disentangle themselves. One finally made it to the door.

<Superb,> the visser muttered as he swaggered into the room. <It now takes two of you to open a door, I see. Yes. Excellent.>

He strode, with graceful Andalite steps, toward the center of the room. He paused briefly to grind a hoof into one of the offending Hork-Bajir's toes. A muffled cry.

<I was,> the visser boomed in public thought-speak, pausing in mid-sentence to turn all four eyes on me, <detained.>

My breathing stopped. My stomach was stone. The darkness in his gaze was terrifying. We had met many times, he and I. But visible through those Andalite eyes was an evil that still struck fear in my heart. Still gripped me with hopelessness and despair.

Perhaps it was the knowledge that this Yeerk had managed something that years of battle had been unable to do: take down the great Elfangor. Stamp out that brave warrior's life. Or maybe looking into Visser Three's eyes made me face the hard reality that despite all our campaigns — the numerous ways we've succeeded in weakening and slowing his invasion of Earth — this Yeerk still stood powerful and strong.

Was he just lucky? Or was he really smarter than we were?

Would he always triumph? Would we never be able to end the invasion? To change the course of humanity's future?

He looked away and released me from his hold.

"Urgent business?" the sub-visser inquired with interest.

<I was detained by the festivities outside, the planning of our new base, the reassigning of duties to more . . . trusted officers. Hmmm.> He scanned the room like the queen of hearts, looking for someone to behead. <And, oh yes,> he

intoned, smoothly reversing the pivot of his stalk eyes to rest on me, <by a small and trivial matter of an Andalite bandit found in the woods. We followed him from here, back to his pitiful shelter.>

I was stunned. Surely this was a bluff. Surely Ax had gotten away. The visser waited, clearly hoping to get a rise out of me.

<We destroyed the scoop, of course.> He paused again. <Touchingly primitive the way Andalites live. You're a claustrophobic species, aren't you? Always craving the open air. Well, your compatriot is now random atoms floating in open air.>

Taylor laughed appreciatively.

I said nothing. And a hawk face shows no emotion.

The visser seemed a little disappointed. <Several other Andalites were found trespassing on community center property. But you can rest assured, Sub-Visser, that they were disposed of.>

No. I refused to believe him. If he'd found anyone in morph, he'd have brought them straight here, to test the ray. We were too valuable as guinea pigs.

Lies.

<Yes. Well.> His stalk eyes drooped slightly. <Shall we proceed to the matter at hand? I think our friend here has waited long enough.>

"Yes, Visser," Taylor answered obsequiously.

<Well, then! Doctors Sinegert and Singh! My two devoted scientists!> He searched the room. <Where are they?>

The door was opened again. This time by a single Hork-Bajir. Two small human-Controllers in white lab coats emerged timidly.

They looked haggard. Like they hadn't slept in days. They gaped at Visser Three, then looked away.

One carried a thick, softbound manual, the other, a large tabletop device. A replica of the three buttons in my glass cube. They set their items cautiously on the table in front of the Visser.

<Are you quite ready?> the Visser asked solicitously.

"Yes, we, I, we . . . Yes."

<Then proceed before I lose all patience!>

They moved quickly, clumsily, shaking.

One of them stumbled, running over to a large object that looked remarkably like the kind of telescope an amateur astronomer might own.

The telescopelike device was aimed at me.

Dr. Singh flipped several switches on the base and shaft of the instrument. The other man appeared to connect power to the three-circle device. The two men then stood together. Their expressions were a disturbing mix of hope and pride and terror.

Together they pressed sweaty palms down onto a large black button.

I would have laughed, if I weren't sick with fear. They were like a pair of hopeful kids in a science fair being judged by a psycho-killer.

The corresponding black circle in my glass cube glowed with an eerie light.

I closed my eyes. Hoping the ray wouldn't kill me, but knowing full well that it could.

I waited.

My body tingled ever so slightly.

Wooomp, wooomp, woomp.

A strained noise, like a helicopter at liftoff, or an old car engine turning over.

Woomp, woomp.

I opened my eyes.

The two little scientists looked unsettled. Their eyes darted nervously from the telescope object to their charts, to their controls, to me.

Then slowly, slowly, they turned their faces to Visser Three.

<A very noisy machine,> the Visser called loudly. <You'll want to work that out now, won't you. Smooth out the details. Fine-tune the instrument . . .>

At this point the scientists' faces grew

flushed. Perspiration beaded on their brows. They flipped rapidly through pages of calculations. One climbed up onto the machine with a wrench and began to peel off the outer body. A wrench. *How high-tech,* I thought.

"I don't understand," one of them said breathlessly. "It is impossible for it not to be working. Impossible." He ran toward me. Stood on tiptoes to peer at me in my cube. I was still a hawk. I had not demorphed. For the very excellent reason that I was not morphed to begin with.

"It must work!"

"Visser . . . it must work. It does work!"

"It works, Visser, it . . . somehow . . ."

Taylor rolled her eyes and sighed.

Visser Three stood completely immobile. A stillness filled the room.

I would not have been surprised to see an actual column of steam rise from his head.

He uttered a single command. <Feed them to the Taxxons. Slowly.>

"No, Visser, no! You don't understand. This must be some sort of Andalite trick. It is inconceivable that the ray should not work." The other one held up a paper brick of calculations and shook it desperately.

"Look through our work, Visser. You will see that it is perfect. That the work is valuable. That we are valuable."

"It's not my fault," a wild-eyed, weeping Dr. Sinegert cried. "It's him! He . . . he's a saboteur! A traitor!"

Visser Three stared hard at me with his main eyes. I stared back. Did he suspect? Did he guess that this game was rigged?

<I don't have time for this,> he said, disgusted. <This Andalite is all yours, Sub-Visser. Make the Andalite demorph. Infest him. I leave the task to you. This is your specialty. Do not disappoint me.> He walked leisurely toward the door.

Hork-Bajir grabbed the scientists. The struggle was brief. A hatch opened in the floor. A grate I had not noticed. From it issued the snorts and sloshings of hungry Taxxons.

"Nooo!"

The Hork-Bajir looked more interested now, as they dangled first one, then the other scientist down into the pit.

I looked away. I could do nothing to shut out their howls of pain. Howls of pain that went on till, at last, with the visser gone, the Hork-Bajir released their hold and dropped the Controllers into the pit.

The floor closed up.

The sub-visser looked shaken. Maybe she guessed that she had just glimpsed her own future.

But I watched her work to recover her strength. Her ruthlessness. Eyes that had held faint traces of pity hardened again.

"You can make this easy, Andalite," she said slowly, deliberately. "Or you can make it . . . horrible." She paused. "It's all up to you."

# CHAPTER 15

She planted her face inches from the glass — uncomfortably close — and stared icily into my hawk eyes. A zoo animal on display. That's how I felt.

"You'll soon be trapped in morph, Andalite," the sub-visser said. "Surely you don't want to live out your life as a bird."

I decided to answer. <I won't give you another Andalite body to infest.>

She looked at me intently for a moment more, as if she found my statement difficult to grasp. The resemblance to Rachel was disturbing. Same proud stance. Same natural, glowing beauty. But I knew the similarity was only skin-deep. Inside, she and Rachel were like night and day.

Or at least night and twilight.

"No, of course you won't." She mocked. "Brave Andalite. Your sense of honor is ridiculous. It will get you nowhere."

She walked across the room with placid determination. Turned her attention to the control panel. It looked like something I'd seen at the modern art museum. Three large circles — maybe six inches in diameter — that stood out vividly against a silver-gray background. Blue, red. And black. That last one I knew. The AMR. But the other two?

She hesitated before the panel, almost like she was afraid. Then suddenly, startlingly, slammed her hand down on the red button. The circle in my cube glowed a deep crimson. I watched it pulsate with color.

And without warning —

<Ahhhhhh!>

It struck like a knife. Staggering, twisting pain that sliced through to my bones.

A dagger . . . twisting . . .

<Ahhhhhhhhhh!>

Sharp bursts of pain knocked the wind out of me. I gasped.

"Demorph," Taylor said.

I was silent. Impossible to respond. To even

think of speaking as the pain seared. Stronger. More intense each second. A high-pitched tone began to ring in my ears.

Couldn't stand it . . . oh, God, the pain!

Stopped.

Gone.

Color drained from the red circle.

I had to look strong. Seem unaffected. Tough. Unbreakable. But I could do nothing but lie there. Lie there and breathe. Breathe.

"Really quite beautiful, isn't it?" she announced. A demented pride shone in her eyes. A look that left no doubt that her lips mouthed the words of the Yeerk within. "Some of our best scientists spent nearly a decade perfecting it. The concept is really quite simple. You see, I have direct, unhindered access to the parts of your brain that control emotion and physical sensation."

She laughed. A pure, girlish sound. She might have been giggling about some boy. "I can make you feel anything I choose. That, in case you couldn't tell, was pain — the lowest setting. I'd like to know what you think. No, really. Be honest. Our scientists appreciate feedback. Especially from a mighty Andalite."

I tried to answer. To appear in control, unaltered. But I still couldn't move. Or summon the strength to conceal the soft, pathetic whimpers I'd never known my hawk voice could make.

"Interesting," mused the sub-visser, assessing my state. "This may be easier than I anticipated. Don't give in too quickly, though. I wouldn't want Visser Three to think anyone could do this job. Ready? One more time? Shall we?"

She hit the red circle again.

I screamed. Screamed and screamed.

My wings trembled, uncontrollable. My beak jerked wildly. Talons clutched at nothing. My bowels failed and I fouled myself.

Indescribable pain. Staggering pain. Pain that ate into me, chewed at my guts, twisted every nerve ending.

Had to make it stop. Had to make it stop!

*Tell her! Tell her! Make it stop, tell her, tell her, tell her!*

Me, the human me, the boy inside kept screaming tell her, tell her!

But the hawk . . . the hawk suffered dumb, helpless. The hawk had no way out. The me that was a bird, the body, the physical me didn't know that there was a cause for the pain.

Didn't know it could make the pain end. And already, for the hawk, the pain had become a fact of life. Reality.

Life was hunger. Life was killing. Life was danger. Life was pain.

The hawk could manage it. Not on a conscious level, of course, but by shutting down.

Keeping alive on a sort of primitive autopilot. Only essential parts of the organism were maintained. No contemplation. No decision. Not even observation. Just survival.

The boy Tobias screamed.

The hawk Tobias had already begun to accept the pain.

# CHAPTER 16

Pain off. Gasping.

Pain on. Screaming.

Off.

On.

Tell her everything!

Pain is normal. Life is pain.

Make it stop!

Go away, human. Go away, little boy. The hawk knows. The predator understands because he understands nothing.

<Let go,> I mumbled to myself. <Let go of yourself.>

"What was that you said?" Taylor asked.

Irrelevant. She was nothing. I was the hawk.

Deeper into the hawk. Go away, weak human boy.

I seemed to stand outside my body. Hawk, human — everything. My mind began to race, the manic frenzy of madness. Up above it all.

A wave of self-pity, followed by a wave of hatred, followed by the unbearable weight of despair. The pain sped everything up. Faster and faster. Panic, fear, sadness.

But somehow . . .

Using the half of me that was equipped to process pain, I was enduring it. *Close down your human mind! It's your only hope,* I told myself. *Focus on the hawk. Focus on the part of you where the pain is less subversive. Less destructive.*

*Sink into your hawk self, Tobias. Deep into your raptor self.*

But the images!

Fragments of memory. Random memory. Flashing uncontrollably across my mind's screen.

Insanity! Madness!

A hyper-speed slide show.

Fleeting. Irrepressible. Dominating my reality and impossible to control. Turn it off. Off!

*The living room was fairly dark. As usual, the shades were drawn. It was about four o'clock and*

he'd just come home. From work as a roofer. His face was tanned and leathery. A beer can in his hand.

"Yeah, so what?" My uncle's voice. Raspy and cold. He sat on the couch, where he spent most of his time. Even spent the night there, too, now. With empty, tired eyes he stared at the TV. He had the scanner on as well. Tuned to the police band. Spouting a stream of mundane reports.

I spoke cautiously. "Well, it's like an honor," I said. "I mean, the committee picked my drawing out from hundreds of entries. Just something I sketched during art class. I had no idea it would make the state show."

I was hoping he would take me to the prizewinners' reception that weekend. Stupid. It wasn't like it was a big deal. But it would have been okay.

"Do you get prize money?" he grumbled casually, not even turning to look at me.

"No," I said, confused.

"No? So then what's it worth? If it won't help pay the bills, what good is it?" He glanced at me patronizingly, then back to the TV. "When I was about your age I already had a job. At this car lot. Washing the cars. All the money went to my mother. All my earnings. Because Dad wasn't around. It was tight . . ." He broke off and leaned back into the couch.

*I stood there at the foot of the stairs, unable to move. I felt the tears welling up in my eyes. Couldn't show him that.*

*I told myself,* No big deal, Tobias. Just some dumb drawing. No big deal.

*To him I said,* "Yeah, well, it was just an idea."

*No answer.*

*I dragged myself upstairs to my room. Walked across to the window. I could cry up here where no one would see.*

*Stupid to cry.*

*Then, through blurry eyes I watched a car pull up to a house across the street. A mom and daughter got out. Walked together to the front door. The little girl was carrying a page smeared with finger paint, crumpling it a little as she walked. The mother stopped, took the picture from her daughter, and carried it into the house like it was the* Mona Lisa.

*It was like someone had set out to shove my life in my face.* Here, Tobias, take a look. Take a look at your life, and at the lives of normal kids. Take a good long look.

*I was alone. I was alone.*

*Where would my strength come from?*

*I raised a hand to brush away the tears.*

*A hand that was . . . fingers that were . . .*

*Tan.*

*Feathers.*

*A wing.*

*I whipped around to face the mirror. Round, expressionless eyes stared back at me.*

<Noooo! Noooooooo!>


"Give it up," Taylor said, her voice dripping sympathy. "Do you think I like doing this?" She laughed her sudden mall-rat giggle. "I will break you. I will. Now demorph, Andalite. Surrender and the pain will end."

# CHAPTER 17

Again and again, the circle glowed. A deep, agonizing red.

Hawk instinct told me to retreat. But to where?

I flapped wildly around the cube. Like an insane chicken in its cage. Nowhere to go!

"Wasted energy," the sub-visser remarked. "You'll wish you'd kept up your strength."

Broken feathers littered the bare bottom of the cube. And had I been more aware, I would have noticed I'd sprained a wing.

I collapsed in a corner, exhausted. Almost destroyed by images of pain and hurt I was powerless to stop.

"Here we go again," Taylor said brightly. "Ready? No? Too bad!"

*Rick Stathis. There, at the top of the hill. Waiting for me on the sidewalk on a frigid winter morning. His breath billowed like an angry bull's. A wide, brawny frame concealed under a heavy black coat. Pale blue eyes searched the block, hoping to see me coming.*

*There was no escape. He would harass me. Punch me. Why did he have it in for me? Why me? I could run the other way. Take the long route to school. But he'd find me eventually. Pound on me extra hard. My stomach churned . . .*

*And there was Aria. The young woman who said she was family. Who said she would give me a home. Care about me, even. Aria. In truth, nothing but a mask — a morph — for Visser Three. Visser Three, plotting my death.*

*I was a dupe. Again.*

*False hope.*

*Never trust . . . never!*

"Demorph, Andalite," the sub-visser repeated, her words a low growl. "Now I'm just getting bored."

Rapid surges of memory now. Inexorable. The cube was hot. Stifling. I struggled to draw a breath.

*"Uhhh! Ahh!"*

*Rick slammed me against the lockers, holding me by the shirt collar.*

*Bam! His fist against my face. I reached up to cup my bloody nose. But it was hard as bone. Curved. Sharp at the tip.*

*I landed on the dusty floor of Jake's attic. Pried the lid off of a Rubbermaid container to eat the food I was too squeamish to kill. Trapped in morph. Forever. Never to morph again. Never to be human again . . .*

Accept it.

I can't!

*Staring out at the crescent moon. The stars. <I want to go home!> I cried in a whisper. But I knew as I spoke I had no idea where home was.*

"You're light-years from home, Andalite." The sub-visser!

*What? Had I spoken aloud?*

"Your people are trillions of miles away. They grow weaker every day. There's no one to save you."

101

*  *  *

*The prey. I was the prey. I was the hunted in every story of animal cruelty Cassie ever told us about.*

*The Canada goose clubbed to death on the golf course. I felt my skull shatter. My confused, terrified cries. Chilling, jubilant grunts of aggression from the boys with baseball bats.*

*The fly lying quivering and scared on the concrete. As two classmates pulled off first one wing, then the other. A scientific experiment, they said. I felt appendages rip off my body wall.*

*The drone of plane engines. A frightening man-made shadow trailing me, tracking me. Responding to every turn I made. I was the wolf. Across untouched snow that glared in the sunlight. Paws pounding. Breathe. Breathe, breathe.*

*I was the wolf I'd seen so many times in the video clip. That wolf, with foam trailing from its mouth. Exhaustion and terror in its eyes. The men in the planes shot everyone else in my pack. From the air. High-powered binoculars and a rifle. Big game hunters who say I ruin their sport. So they will chase me down. Chase me until I can't run anymore. And fall, heart exploding, onto the plain. Victim of slaughter.*

*Better for the wolf who cannot fathom the evil depths in their predators' hearts. Who sees this* merely in terms of nature's hierarchy. Man is smarter. Man has run wolf down the way wolf runs down the caribou.

But I am wolf and human. I see more.

Visser Three towered huge and horrific above an injured Elfangor. Closed him in monstrous jaws. The Visser's shrill cries of victory rang in my head. Elfangor. The father I never knew. My link to everything strong, enduring, and good in the universe.

Murdered.

Anger boiled inside me. A rage whose power made me shake. Energy that rose up and took control. Infested me. I will end him! I will end that Yeerk! The hatred carved away my insides. Scarred me, scraped me clean.

Leave me free! I pleaded. But the anger wouldn't go.

And I shot toward the earth, in full dive. Opened my wings quickly, to slow my descent. Glide in. Glide faster! Ready, now! Talons strained forward, outstretched. Closed over the prey. Punctured the skin. Into the heart. Around the skull. Too efficient for the squirrel to scream.

Yeeeeeeee! Yeeeeee! A bone-chilling wail. What? Hadn't I killed it? Back up. Up. Power hard to reach the trees. Blood dripping from my talons. A warm, wriggling body flailing to break free. To live.

"You tiresome bird! Demorph!"


*The hawk in me tightened its hold. The human in me screamed. And screamed again. I don't want to do this. A life extinguished in an instant. Agony. Death. So that I could survive.*

*I looked down. There were no talons there. No. Only human fingers. Blood-covered fingers. Strangled by my human hands!*

*<Noooo!>*

*And I shot toward the earth, in full dive. Spread my wings wide, to slow my descent. Easy, easy. Now! Talons sprang forward. And reached.*

*"Gilalll. Ahhh!"*

*The Hork-Bajir grabbed his eyes in anguish. Blinded. I rose in the air to reach sufficient altitude to dive and strike again. And as I flew, I felt the burden of a thousand wounds, each one fresh and vivid in my mind. Weighing me down.*

*How can you carry such a weight? All the pain I had inflicted. Seemingly inevitable. Perhaps avoidable. Strikes made by me. A hawk. A warrior. A ruthless kid.*

*One deafening shriek, comprised of the voices of all those I had faced in combat over-*

*powered me. Shook me. Hork-Bajir. Taxxon. Rabbit. Squirrel. Human.*

*My head filled with screams. Everything red. Excruciating. Endless, endless. Violent images rushing past like the landscape out a car window. Was this payback? Was that it?*

And then:
Silence.
Peace.
Slowly, completely, the agony drained away.
The red circle flickered, and dimmed.

# CHAPTER 18

"Arrrgh!" The sub-visser ran at the nearest Hork-Bajir and gave him a shove. He grunted, but knew better than to respond further.

"I'm a fool!" she raged suddenly, inexplicably. "Of course the pain ray can't break you! You're using your morph as a shield. Any sentient creature would long since have wilted from this much pain. Whatever ugly bird you are now isn't sentient. It can't be! You would never have lasted . . ."

She flipped rapidly through a manual the scientists had left on the console. She stopped on a page near the end, smiled, read some more, then slapped the book shut and tossed it across the table.

"It's all about contrast, don't you think?" Taylor asked. "That's the way life is, eh? You don't know pain unless you know pleasure. You don't know what it is to be strong unless you've been weak. Isn't that right, Andalite?"

<I don't know,> I managed to say. <Let me know . . . if you ever become strong.>

"You think I'm weak now?" she shrilled. "I have you in my power, Andalite. You call me weak? No. No, I was weak. Now I'm strong. I know the difference. And when you submit, you will know the difference, too."

Her hand moved over the blue circle. She hesitated, seemingly savoring her moment. Then she slammed down her fist.

The circle glowed. A soulful, soothing indigo.

And in my mind I heard laughter. Peals of joyous, human laughter. My own.

*I bounced wildly on a trampoline. Out of control. Walked home from school barefoot, squishing cool spring mud between my toes. Felt a sugar cube melt on my tongue. Discovered that soft spot behind a cat's ear that made Dude close his eyes in ecstasy.*

"Pleasure, Andalite. Fun, isn't it? Remembering happy days back on your filthy planet? Are you recalling happy times, running across the grass? Of course, you are. Up and down, Andalite. Pain and pleasure. I will take you into madness, Andalite."

Pleasure.

The blue button was pleasure: intense, continuous, out of control.

The hawk didn't know pleasure. Satisfaction, yes. The satisfaction of a good kill, the meal that followed. But happiness?

*Don't leave me, Tobias the hawk. I know what she will do, I know what the foul Yeerk will do, but oh, oh, no sadness, no fear, all gone.*

*Happy! Joyful!*

Such happiness. Not for a hawk. Pleasure was human domain. Purely human.

*I raced through the garden, stopping at a raspberry bush. Frothy ocean waves crashed against the rocks. A fairweather wind tousled my hair. I picked a berry and ate it. So sweet on my tongue. Sublime. The sun on my face.*

*"Young man!" From the hilltop house, perched like a lighthouse above the cove, came an elderly woman. Graying hair. A strong, deep voice. Of course! These berries were hers. This*

*garden. I was an intruder. I turned to run. But no, something kept me there. A kindness in her eyes.*

*Into a kitchen washed with light. Walls painted warm tones of yellow. Deep shades of blue. Cozy, comforting heat enveloped me as I neared the stove. And the aromas! Hot cider. Homemade cinnamon rolls. Raspberry tart.*

*When no one else cared, Professor Powers fed me and told me stories. Gave me the illusion of home.*

"You have at most twelve minutes left in morph. Maybe less! Are you a fool? Do you want to live out the rest of your life eating roadkill? Never to know such pleasure, such happiness again?"

Sudden, hideous pain!

Pain, and no hawk to save me. Agony and no escape!

No, no, no, no, I was all alone, me, just me, just Tobias, the boy.

Pain as if my body was being fed into a meat grinder. Unbearable!

*Hawk! Come back, save me, protect me!*

\*     \*     \*

"Ticktock, ticktock, the Andalite will be a bird forever, ticktock." She was close by. I couldn't see her, my eyes, red with my own blood, the veins broken.

"Time's almost up, Andalite. You'll never run free again. Never use that fantastic tail of yours. You'll die, so soon. How long does a hawk live?"

*Rachel?*

*No, no, the sub-visser.*

*I want you with me, to be part of me, my life, not to die a bird, not to die for nothing.*

*Rachel?*

*Rachel! Rachel!*


*I was listening to the waves crash over the rocks.*

*A late spring morning. The thinning fog beaded on my face as I buzzed the shoreline, then turned inland. Glided over a baseball field, subdivisions, a strip mall. A familiar route to my destination: Rachel's window.*

*I coasted in for a landing on her ledge and knocked gently against the glass with my beak.*

*Dink. Dink.*

*I waited, heart pounding from exertion. Her comforter rustled. Feet padded across the floor. And there she was. Framed by the dappled sunlight of early morning.*

"Hey, you," she whispered with a smile.

<Ready for some fun?>

"You know it, Soaring Hawk."

The others say morphing makes even Rachel look bad and I can understand. It strains the definition of beauty. But to me, she looked natural and strong. I liked watching her change. She was an eagle now.

And down into a dive!

<Yahhhhh!> We both screamed. Rotating wildly as we plummeted toward Earth in free fall from an insane height. The sand and hills and wharves raced toward us as we dropped. An awesome rush.

<Now, now!> I cried, giddy.

We spread our wings, like parachutes. Caught the air just above a whitecap breaking on shore. We found a thermal and caught the free ride. Up and up and up again. Circle after circle. World's greatest carnival ride.

<There is nothing, nothing like this, Tobias!> she shouted, awed by the sheer joy of flying.

We weren't a hawk and eagle on this morning. We were two humans. Rejoicing in the greatest pleasure we'd ever known. Enjoying the gift Elfangor had given us. Rising toward the brilliant, dazzling sun.

\*      \*      \*

"My patience is about to end," Taylor said quietly.


Pain.
Pleasure.
Pain.
Who was I? Where?


I lay on my back in the cube, staring into an interrogation light.

The sun. I watched it burn and shimmer. Intense and warming.

ARE YOU HAPPY, TOBIAS?

I remembered the Ellimist. The voice that came from everywhere and nowhere.


*And I flapped down from the beam in Cassie's barn to see the clothes Rachel picked for Ax's day at school. Smiling at Marco's sarcasm: "Rachel, he looks like he's going to the country club to play polo. He's like a bully magnet. Even I want to beat him up."*

*And Ax: "Yes, I am fully human. Mun. Hyew-mun. Human. Huh-yew-mun."*

*Then, the time I stood next to Cassie. Over a large flowerpot on her back porch. We'd all come* over to see them. Two baby rabbits. *"Parsley"* and *"Pansy"* Marco had named them.

*"Go ahead, Tobias. It's your turn."* Cassie smiled encouragement. I stepped forward with my lettuce leaf. Reached a hand over those two tiny, vulnerable little lives. Trusting now, because we'd nurtured them.

*And the moonlit night I galloped across the field behind Cassie's barn. Ax just behind me. He said the grass there was of superior quality. Richer soil.*

*Skr-eet. Skr-eet. Skr-eet.*

*A deafening alarm. Blinking lights.*

*I closed my eyes again. Still feeding with Ax. Still crushing lush grass underhoof.*

I felt the pleasure ray shutting down. I realized I was in the cube.

"Your time is up. Do you understand that? You can never escape your morph. You will be a bird till you die."

Who said that? Rachel? Taylor, the sub-visser? Me?

113

# CHAPTER 19

"You vile little bird!" she shrieked. "Who are you? To sacrifice your body! Do you realize what you've done?"

Still in a stupor I rolled over and saw her pacing in front of my cube, thinking visibly. Running through her options. If she couldn't present Visser Three with a new Andalite-Controller, what was left?

Her fear was obvious. It twisted her face. It made her breath come short and fast.

While she'd tortured me her desperation had grown.

"The Andalite bandits. Give me their location!" She stamped her foot on the floor like a

114

frustrated, tired child. "Tell me where they are. I demand it! Where are your friends?"

I was silent.

"Your childish loyalty is amusing. But you'll learn, Andalite." She spoke the words bitterly and with emphasis. "You'll learn that it's foolish to protect your friends. Friends always betray you."

I answered instinctively, forgetting to keep up my guard. <Mine wouldn't.>

"Oh, wouldn't they?" she snapped. She walked back to the table. Toward the three-color device. I could tell she had more to say, but she bottled it, and said simply, "I pity your innocence."

Right then I had only one thought. If I could distract her, maybe the torture would stop. If I could draw her out, maybe she'd forget to press the button. For a moment. At least for a moment.

<What would you know about disloyalty?> I said, desperate.

She stiffened. "You do not ask the questions, Andalite!" she roared. "I ask. You answer."

Her hand hovered dangerously above the red circle.

I couldn't take any more. I couldn't. The hawk was defeated. The human, defeated. Me, whatever I was, I was defeated.

115

No more. No more pain. No more memory.

Milk-white fingers brushed the button's surface.

Get her to talk! Appeal to her sense of power. Her pride . . .

<You're very pretty,> I blurted out. Almost immediately I wished I hadn't. Complimenting this monster made me ill. <Pretty, by what I understand of human standards.>

But she froze.

Her fingers lifted from the button —

"Yes," she said, "I know."

— and touched the side of her face. "There was a time when I . . . this body . . . was the prettiest and most popular girl in her school. When I had a party, everyone . . ."

I'd struck a nerve. Keep going. Keep her hand from the button.

<Everyone what?>

"Shut up, Andalite. Be silent, and suffer."

<He's going to kill you. Feed you to the Taxxons. Or do the job himself.>

That stopped her.

<You've failed him. Visser Three won't tolerate failure. You know that. But I guess that's life in the happy little Yeerk Empire.>

She looked hard at me. She knew I was trying to provoke her. She knew I was trying to delay the pain.

She also knew I was right.

<I won't give in,> I said. <Do you know why?>

"No."

<Because if I surrender, you'll live. And if I resist, you'll die. And I want you to die.>

# CHAPTER 20

The sub-visser snorted derisively. "He needs me. I'm his expert on humans."

<He has lots of human-Controllers.>

"Not like me!" she yelled, flying into a sudden rage. "I'm a voluntary, do you not know that? This girl, this human, chose this life, chose to invite me in to take control! Why? Why? Because she'd seen humans as they truly were. She chose us over her own people. Why? Because humans are weak and petty and stupid and we will rule them all, we will make them ours, all of them!"

She was shaking. From rage? From fear?

<A human would have to be very weak and foolish to turn against her own,> I said.

I had no idea what I was saying. No idea what

kind of twisted person I was dealing with. She seemed to make no sense. I was throwing anything out there. Saying anything. Anything to keep her going, talking. Away from the button.

"Weak? Foolish? When I . . . when she walked down the hall at school, there wasn't a boy who didn't dream she was his." She came right up to my cube. Her breath steamed the glass. "Not a girl who didn't wish she were her. She was homecoming queen. Tennis champion. Student-body president. She was the princess, and the school was her court."

What was going on? I'd never heard a Yeerk talk this way. This was Taylor I was hearing. At least as much as the Yeerk inside her.

<That doesn't add up,> I pressed. <Not to becoming a voluntary Controller.>

She ignored me. Her eyes scanned the air as she searched her mind for the past.

"There was nothing she couldn't do! Had it all. Humans have pleasures that Yeerks . . . a different world of senses, of sight and sound and touch and . . . nothing she couldn't have! The memories, when we first came together, I went through them all, of course, you have to when you first infest a new host, and they were so . . ."

Suddenly, she fell to her knees on the cold, barren concrete.

"Then the fire. She was alone that night. My

119

parents . . . her parents, her parents . . . were out, at some party." Taylor shook her head and her blond hair glimmered. "I still don't know how it happened. How it could have happened! When I, she, woke up the house was blazing. Flames attacking my door. Crackling outside my window. Smoke everywhere. I couldn't escape!"

She covered her face with her hands. Hands that I had seen change. Hands I knew were artificial.

*Keep her talking, Tobias. Buy time. It's all you have.*

<What happened then?> I said, my voice soft, low.

"Terrible," she said. "Horrible. The pain. You can't . . . well, yes, maybe you can imagine. We lost our left arm. Her right leg. And my face . . . some came to see me in the hospital, some friends. Never again, after that. Word went around. She's a monster. She's hideous. One day I was queen. The next day, nothing."

<But The Sharing, they cared?> I chanced.

"They held out friendship. Hope. In her darkest hour, they made me believe that her life wasn't over. That I had a future. Then came the offer. If I . . . she . . . would enter their center circle — take advantage of everything they had to give me — they would repair her body. They had their own members' hospital, they said. Incredibly advanced technology. I would be whole again. I would be what I once had been!"

Taylor scrambled to her feet. She plastered her hands against the glass of my cube and stared at me. Her glare was intense, compelling. As if she were trying to make me understand.

"Maybe it seemed a little weird at first." She slammed her palms against the cube and I shuddered. "But all I could think about were the kids at school. I hated them for forgetting me. All she wanted was for things to be the way they had been. I wanted to be envied. Envied. Do you understand!" she demanded. "I wanted all of that, all the memories, the sweet, perfect memories, I wanted to live that life."

*She's crazy,* I realized. *She's insane. The Yeerk. The girl. The line between them all confused.*

*Hawk. Boy.*

*Yeerk. Girl.*

I had a terrifying moment of understanding. Pity. To be the human girl desperate, terrified, alone, all alone, needing someone to look at her without cringing. To be the Yeerk, hungry for sensations that were so intense, so powerful compared to the dull, blind life of a slug.

"I took the deal." Taylor laughed dryly. "Two Controllers helped me, in my wheelchair, I waited down in the pool, not knowing what host,

I'd only ever been Hork-Bajir before. I allowed myself to be infested, she opened herself to me, willingly. Until that moment, until I was lying on my stomach, my head held over the surface of the pool, she hadn't known, of course, how could she? How could I?"

Taylor's eyes closed briefly.

"This girl, this Taylor person, this insignificant injured girl wasn't my goal, of course, I was a sub-visser, I was slated for a host who held a vital position. My mother, the chief of police. I betrayed her, of course. Helped them take her involuntarily."

Her eyes flickered. Shame? Surely not. Not from the Yeerk. But the human? The human who was half of this split personality? Maybe.

"I didn't want her, the older woman. I wanted these memories. I wanted the life I knew would be mine when the Yeerks, when my people, had repaired the body. And now, I am beautiful once again," she said triumphantly. "But look at you! Look at what you've become! How pathetic your hawk body is! A nothing creature. All for nothing."

<And now you hurt others to make up for your suffering?>

She was silent.

<Who are you?>

Her face twitched. Her eyes bored in on mine.

<Who are you?> I asked again.

"I am a sub-visser of the Yeerk Empire."

<No. You're a weak, misguided human girl. And you are also insane.>

She hung her head. For a long time she said nothing. Looked at nothing.

Then, at last, she raised her face to me and smiled.

"Then join me in my madness, Andalite," she said and sent my body and mind reeling into hell.

# CHAPTER 21

The blue button glowed. I laughed crazily. Like being tickled, I couldn't stop.

And then:

<Ahhh!> Punched in the gut. The red circle screamed.

Blue. Giddy, laughing hysterically. Eating ice cream.

Red. Slapped in the face. Struck with a two-by-four. Surgery without anesthesia.

I flew up, flung myself at the glass. <Stop!> I cried. I wanted it to end. If she wouldn't stop, I would end it myself. By ending me.

I threw myself against the side of the cube. My beak cracked. Splinters of pain electrified my face.

The blue button lit up and I was laughing madly.

The red button roared and I was gripped with grief. My aunt's voice: *I don't want him! He's nothing to me. Where does Loren get off dumping him here?*

Again I shot toward the wall.

"I've got you now!" Taylor cried.

<Stop!> I cried again, barely able to speak. I fell into a corner. The room was dimming quickly now. The light that had seemed so bright was just a dull glow. Disappearing.

Disappearing . . .

Alone. I was alone!

Ax, Jake, Cassie, Marco. How could they do this to me?! Abandon me here! I hate everyone who isn't here. Who isn't going through this with me.

If only Rachel were here. Rachel . . .

No! She's dead. Dead or trapped. All of us. All the ones I love . . .

<Ahhhh!>

A pain! Greater than anything!

What did this lunatic girl want from me? What did she want? She no longer cared what she got out of me. This was pain for its own sake. Hurt for no purpose but to hurt.

She would kill me. No, no, she wouldn't! She would keep me alive, alive in this inferno.

<I'll tell you,> I screamed. <Yes, I'll tell you! Ax . . . in the woods. Cassie. Jake. Marco. All just human kids. Anything . . . anything to make it end!>

Did she hear? Did she not hear my thought-speak cry?

She slammed her fist on the pain button.

<I'll tell you! No! I'll tell you!>

No sound coming from me. Or did she not hear? Or was I not making a sound? Was I even still alive?

Down, swirling down. The world . . .

Dimming . . .

Death. Was this death?

*And I was walking in the woods. A path lined with trees whose upper boughs met in cathedral arches. Near the school. After a play we'd put on. "Is your father here tonight?" the teacher had asked.*

*"Yeah. Where's your dad?" said a classmate.*

*I followed the trail through the woods. My heart so full. I stopped at a clearing. A point stuck up out of the dirt, gleamed in the moonlight, caught my eye. I dug in the surrounding earth, trying to free the object. Deeper and deeper.*

*A hard, scythe-shaped blade. I held it before me. Why did it seem so familiar? So much a part*

of me? I looked beyond it into the evening sky.
And froze.

Two moons cast a warm yellow light over the
woods. Over thick asparagus-spear trees.

What!

This wasn't Earth! This was . . .

The moonlight brightened to a strong and
dazzling brilliance. It compelled my gaze. I
couldn't look away. I didn't want to.

<Tobias,> he said.

I started, scared. The light faltered.

<Don't be afraid.>

A broad face came into focus. A familiar face.
An Andalite.

I watched as a tail arced upward. Curved
slowly over his back and moved toward me.

A shiver. As the cool flat of his blade pressed
against my forehead. It was electric. Like nothing
I've felt before or since.

A new surge of memories! But how? How can
they be memories when I haven't lived them?
They're new to me, though they seem like mine.
No, these were not my own.

They were . . .

# CHAPTER 22

<*Pull up! Pull up! War-Prince Elfangor!*> An urgent transmission from the commander of the fighter squadron. On the view screen: a Desbadeen tanker in the distinctive figure eight design.

<*Positive burn cut to zero. Still-speed compensators engaged.*> The fighter's computer voice broadcast thought-speak data with admirable calm. <*Large alien obstruction ahead. Two seconds to impact.*>

*Every particle of my body focused on the hole of the figure eight. Guide the ship through that opening. Clearing it was my only hope.*

*The computer voice:* <*Required clearance not found. Warning. Warning. Escape pod activated!*>

*I fumbled wildly for the clasps. The sides of the ship scraped and erupted into fire. Searing heat scorched my arms and flank.*

*Ka-choomp!*

*The ship ejected me into space. But I couldn't clear the Desbadeen craft! The gray wall of steel filled my vision!*

*<Ahhhh!>*

*I hit like a bullet.*

*Rods of fire in every bone. My body tossed from wall to wall as the pod hurtled uncontrollably through space. Stars streaked the blackness. The Dome ship. Too far . . . too far. I was alone.*

Red colored the air. Screams and bellowing filled my head. The battle raged on the Taxxon home world.

"Sssseeeeeyaaa!"

*A hundred Taxxon teeth bit down on my leg.*

"Sssreeee!"

*Another mouth sliced into my forearm.*

*I had to fight! Kill to survive!*

*Sshhhwing! I whipped my tail up from my rear and sliced clean through his belly.*

"Skkkreeeee-eeeeeee!" *A cry of horror I will never forget. My first kill.*

*I looked at the second Taxxon. Into those gel-*

atinous eyes. Those who say you can't read emotion in Taxxon eyes are fools. I saw terror there. A plea for life. My hearts pounded. Nausea.

"Sssssnnnnaaaaa!"

I cut a gaping hole in its side. It released my arm. Fell to the ground, shrieking in agony. I turned, and with a retching noise expelled the morning's grass.

So this was war.


I stood on the grass near the Dome ship's lake. Stared into the crystals that grew up from the water. A seductive, hypnotic green.

Loren. I longed to have her here next to me. To hear her say my name. To see our son.

I performed a ritual for his safety and health.

Five years since the Ellimist returned me to my proper time. Five years since I left my life on Earth to resume Andalite form and honor my duty.

And I thought of my future. Would I accomplish anything in this fight for freedom? Was the struggle, the pain, the loneliness endured in vain? Would I die before I defeated the enemy?


The icy tail blade against my forehead cooled my fevered mind. Kept me alive.

\*     \*     \*

*<You're not alone in your suffering. You may die, Tobias, but never alone. You are one in a legion of great warriors. Valiant Andalites who have died for freedom. Your lineage is courage and bravery. If you live, you carry our torch. A burden carried by many. A singular honor . . .>*

The brightness began to fade.

A final, overwhelming surge of things lived by Elfangor. Warrior. Intellectual. Oh, how he had lived! Endured. Accomplished. A sense of purpose. Things I couldn't comprehend. Things I could. Things I might become.

Dimmer and dimmer. To a pinpoint of light. I felt my body shudder and I knew that I was dying. That pinpoint was life.

<I'll make the Andalite filth talk!> Visser Three's far-off, threatening voice struck my ear.

*Hold to the pinpoint. Hold!*

Just as the light was about to extinguish, I felt the torture device flicker, and stop. The pinprick of light began to grow. Until at last I no longer looked into darkness, but saw the cube around me. I was flattened against the floor. Defeated, but alive.

The last, fading strain of Elfangor's voice:

*<Out of a respect for life, you have to endure.>*

# CHAPTER 23

< This will make him talk.>

The thought-speak voice of Visser Three.

He stood behind Taylor. Her face was blank. No emotion. Then I saw her glance down at the floor. At the hatch that opened onto the starved Taxxons below.

Two Hork-Bajir banged through the door just behind the Visser. They carried a thick pole slung through a large wire cage. In the cage, a bald eagle.

An eagle!

Rachel! It must be Rachel!

The visser could hardly contain his enthusiasm.

<This eagle was found near the community center. How audacious and foolhardy of your

friends, Andalite! For we have seen the bandits use this morph before.>

He swaggered confidently toward my cube. Pointed a long Andalite finger at the eagle.

<Tell me all you know. Or I will feed your fellow Andalite to the Taxxons.>

<No,> I whispered. <No, I . . .> I started to speak. I struggled to focus my eyes. To see past the leaden veil of fatigue.

The bird was badly injured. With a broken wing. Blood ran down its leg. Feathers matted and missing from the chest.

I breathed.

<Speak! Or he dies!> The visser roared.

<You'll get nothing from me, Yeerk,> I said.

<You dare defy me! You dare resist!> He swung his tail blade and whipped his stalk eyes savagely. <Now!> he screamed.

<You want me to open the hatch?> Taylor asked.

<I've made my own arrangements,> the visser said coldly.

The hatch remained closed. Instead the door opened and two slobbering Taxxons, monstrous centipedes, skittered in on their rows of needle legs.

Red, globular eyes wiggled anxiously. Long, thin tongues smacked hundreds of razor-sharp teeth.

<Open the cage!>

"Shouldn't we torture it, Visser?" Taylor asked, her voice tight with excitement. "This one might talk. We might get results."

<No! This one will die! That one,> he pointed at me, <will talk.>

A Hork-Bajir undid the latch. The Taxxons rushed the cage, knocking it over in their eagerness. The eagle flapped and squawked, but it was over in a few bites.

I was coming back to life. I even tried to rise. The visser peered in at me, disappointed. But no longer in an eager rage.

<Kill this one, too,> he said flatly. <But do it slowly. See if you can, at least, do this much well,> sneered the visser as he turned and left the room.

This would be it. I knew that. I would die in the next round of torture. I would try to die well. I braced myself for the attack, took a last look around the room. It was just me, the sub-visser, and twelve hulking Hork-Bajir.

And . . .

I stumbled back.

<Already so weak!> the sub-visser mocked. <And we haven't even begun!>

No way. I had to be hallucinating. My frazzled mind was playing a trick on me. This couldn't be real.

I knocked my head against the glass just to make sure I was conscious. I was. So what I saw growing up from the floor, behind the sub-visser, was no mirage!

Silently, unseen by all but me.

A single Andalite emerging from flea morph!

# CHAPTER 24

A smooth blue chin emerged from piercing, sucking mouthparts. Andalite arms sprouted from tiny flea legs.

Ax?

Another hallucination. It had to be.

And yet, there he was, rising up from behind a solid dozen Hork-Bajir warriors.

<Tobias,> he whispered. <Do not let them see you staring.>

Ax against twelve Hork-Bajir? Impossible.

<The others jumped off outside,> he said, as if he'd read my mind. <They will be along shortly. As soon as I open the door. We morphed fleas to travel on the body of the doomed bald eagle from Cassie's barn.>

Could I believe my eyes? My frazzled mind?

<The Chee have secured an escape route,> he added.

"Hear me, Andalite," Taylor said to me. "You've caused me to lose the visser's trust. You may well have destroyed me. And now, I will make you pay. Oh, yes. I've given you pain. I've given you pleasure. You've experienced them in succession. But never both at once. I will tear your mind apart!"

I tensed. Praying that I would survive.

Fwapp!

Ax's tail slapped the door handle.

Fwapp!

The nearest Hork-Bajir went down, not even knowing what had hit him.

Sudden explosions of violence. A flash of Marco, huge and powerful in gorilla morph. A tiger, slashing. Hork-Bajir running. The wolf, so fast, so accurate with its dangerous white teeth.

And the bear.

The huge, slashing, bellowing, death-dealing grizzly bear in a rage.

Rachel.

She looked at me. Even with dim bear vision she could guess what had happened to me.

Five Hork-Bajir were dropped in as many seconds, three of them from swift, brutal encounters with Rachel.

Marco shoved Taylor rudely aside. He had no way of knowing who she was. What she was.

"A gorilla!" she yelped.

<Oh, it's a gorilla, all right, lady!> Marco yelled. <But this here is the new, improved gorilla morph. Now with tools.>

He reached the wall and heaved a grappling hook into the air. Over a steel beam. It clanked and connected.

"Stop him!" Taylor yelled. "Stop him!"

<Climb, man! Climb!> Jake coached.

Three Hork-Bajir dashed after Marco. Jake let rip a fearsome roar.

The remaining row of warriors lunged. Seized on Jake with blades flashing and harsh shouts roared in the Hork-Bajir tongue.

"*Ghafrash!! Gulferch* Andalites!"

But they hadn't checked their backs.

A blur of Andalite tail blade and one was down. A snarl and chomp of wolf jaws and another fell to the floor, cradling his leg. That left five. Five dazzling, muscular machines of destruction.

Marco leaped at the wall. Feet against it, hands clutching the rope, he climbed quickly toward the ceiling. Nostrils flaring. His small eyes widening as he strained in rhythmic grunts toward his goal.

<The girl!> I yelled.

Taylor was running for the weapon cabinet, torture device in hand. Cassie grabbed her heel. Yanked back and forth.

"Get off me! Yahhh!" She slammed Cassie across the muzzle with the control device.

Cassie yipped and lost her hold.

Marco was swinging from conduit to conduit now. Flying across the ceiling like a giant monkey in the rain forest canopy. Two Hork-Bajir were in pursuit, just one swing behind. Another midway up the rope. It wasn't hard to tell they had evolved as tree-dwellers. Marco grabbed for a smaller pipe.

<Waaaaahhh!>

It was no pipe at all! Just a bundle of wires, unsecured. They began to snap under Marco's weight.

Kkkkkkeeehh! Kkkkeh!

Sparks flew as the wires broke. But Marco held on, clutching the cable like a vine, swinging desperately to reach the cube. One of the Hork-Bajir dangled from a nearby beam. He raised his elbow blades into position and slashed the wire.

Zzzzzzz. Kkkkkkk. Zzzzzz.

A blue flash!

A visible charge of controlled lightning arced from the wires to the Hork-Bajir. He shook and trembled in the grisly grips of electrocution. I looked away. He dropped to the floor.

Thwoomp!

Two mammoth gorilla feet struck the top of my cube. It swayed violently and smacked me against the wall.

<Sorry, man!> Marco yelled as he wrapped a giant hand around the steel cable that suspended the cube. <But there's a time for delicacy and this ain't it!> He tightened thick fingers around a bolt head, securing the top of my cube to the cable. He twisted with all his might, trying to loosen the connection that held me a helpless, dangling prisoner.

BOOM! BOOM!

BOOM! BOOM!

Four clawlike Hork-Bajir feet etched the top of the cube. Sent it bobbing out of control.

<Ahhh!> Marco scrabbled to find his balance. The Hork-Bajir flailed, looking for a hold.

*"Gilaaaaaaa!"*

One slipped off, unsuccessful.

Floomp. Tasssshh!

He crashed to the floor. Green-blue blood began to ooze from his chest. Impaled on his own tail blade!

We were an out-of-control pendulum. How could the other Hork-Bajir maintain?!

And then I saw how. He had found a hold. And the hold was Marco's flank.

Marco fell to his knees on the cube. His face,

contorted with agony, teeth bared, pressed onto the glass.

<Ahhhhhhh!> he screamed.

The Hork-Bajir, eyes bulging from strain, muscles flexing powerfully, struck again.

Ptt. Ptt. Ptt.

Red droplets began to spatter the top of the glass. The Hork-Bajir had slashed and embedded a wrist blade deep in Marco's flesh. The more they struggled, the more we bobbed. An unanchored raft.

Pttpttpttptt. The blood splattered more quickly now.

<Marco! Forget me. Just free yourself. He's killing you!>

Marco grunted, agonized. He continued to work on the bolts.

<No,> he gasped.

Two Hork-Bajir had Ax pinned into a corner. Another two slashed mercilessly at Jake. He swiped back with lightning-fast claws, but he was a bloody mess. Missing an ear.

<Marco!> Cassie screamed.

The sub-visser spun 180 degrees. From the weapon cabinet to the room's center. She extended her arm. Her hand clutched a Dracon beam. Aimed . . .

<Marco!> I screamed.

Directly above my head.

At Marco!

BOOM! BOOM!

BOOM! BOOM!

Two more Hork-Bajir landed on the cube.

"Arrrgh!" Taylor shouted. Cassie leaped and knocked her down. Too late!

She fired.

# CHAPTER 25

TSEEEEW!

Dracon fire.

Keeeew!

And a snap. The cable, vaporized, just below Marco's hand!

The cube. Free! The floor rushing up . . .

KABLAMMMMM!

The cube smashed the floor in a thunder crack.

*"Ghalaaaa!"*

<Yeeaaaaaahhhh!>

Screams of confusion. Pain.

Shards of glass shot out from the impact like shrapnel. Drawing blood indiscriminately.

Wumph.

The dead weight of a Hork-Bajir arm collapsed onto me and held me down, my back to the floor. I looked up through a hole, a cylinder burned clean through his upper arm by Dracon fire!

Marco dangled from the red-hot wire. Flesh and hair began to sizzle.

<Hraaaaahh!> Thought-speak and gorilla fused in one wrenching bellow. A primal scream. He couldn't take it! He dropped. Onto a bed of gouging glass that cut and snapped under his weight. Another roar.

Pain wracked my body. As though the impact had fractured every bone. But I was conscious. *Morph! Focus!* The snarls and snorts of battle throbbed in my ears as violence raged around me. I felt the changes begin.

Suddenly the Hork-Bajir body was lifted and thrown aside. I was startled, vulnerable. I stopped the morph, twin Andalite arms budding from my chest.

Blond hair glittered. Spotlights. An iron-strong hand closed over my seven small fingers. Crushing them!

The sub-visser!

She yanked me across the piercing glass. Began to drag me across the floor. But then let me drop and ran back toward the destroyed cube like she'd forgotten something.

<Help!> My voice issued as a dry hiss. Jake and Ax, two-on-five with Hork-Bajir, couldn't hear my cry. The sub-visser picked through glassy rubble and found what she was looking for: the miniature copy of the control panel. With the larger control under one arm and the smaller one in her hand, she headed for me again.

<Help!> I called again, desperate. But I was too weak! Cassie couldn't hear me. I watched as she leaped off the table onto Hork-Bajir shoulders, knocking him down.

Only Marco saw me. He moved to run, but collapsed to the ground in a spasm of pain.

I tried to force the morph. Faster! Where was the tail! The blade!

I couldn't keep my focus. I flapped pathetically with my half-wing, half-arms. Beat at the air and scratched across the floor with exhausted legs. But I couldn't get away.

<Ahhhh!>

I felt the red circle cut into my back. Cripple me. Then stop. She was striking at me again with the torture device. But why now?

Again she clutched my delicate Andalite fingers. Out through the door she dragged me. Onto a sort of balcony. Maybe forty feet long, but very narrow. Not more than four feet wide. Projected out off the rock face. Running into a small tunnel at the far end. An observation deck? In an underground network of narrow tunnels? A putrid, earthy odor filled my lungs. A stench I . . .

"Ahhh!" A loud, shrill yell as she exerted herself to swing me up over the railing. Up in an arc I sailed, her fingers still gripping my own.

Bam! I slammed against the outside wall of the balcony.

<Uhhh!> Pain rattled my bones for the hundredth time. I looked down.

The Yeerk pool.

That vast cavern the size of three Astrodomes. A Yeerk complex underground. Beneath the foundations of half our city. Storage and control center buildings. Docked spacecraft. Diverse alien species moving rapidly about their business, united in a common goal: the conquest of humanity. And there, at the center, was the pool itself. Sludgy, leaden liquid teaming and churning with Yeerk slugs. In their natural state. Vulnerable there, and there only.

"I don't know what you are!" the sub-visser yelled to make herself heard over the shrieks of protestation from the involuntary controllers caged at the Yeerk pool's edge, and the less horrific acoustic wash of the dome. "I don't know what power you possess, that you can morph beyond the two-hour limit." An inhuman hatred coated her words. "But I know that I don't care. You will die! Die! Die!"

She tightened her grip until the bones in my fingers cracked audibly. And then, she released her hold.

# CHAPTER 26

"Die! Die!" she shrieked.

But I clung to her.

With weak, shaking, half-formed Andalite fingers, I held on. Dangled from the end of Taylor's artificial arm. Some hundred meters from the nearest platform below.

"Let go!" she screeched, struggling to shake off my fingers. "Let go, you filthy grass eater!"

Still holding the smaller control device in her other hand, she moved to pry off my hold. The device slipped out of her hand.

I looked down and saw the control device replica still falling. Falling.

*Cooonk!*

It hit a metal storage building and ricocheted off the wall of the lower landing.

I didn't hear it splash. But I watched as it landed in the Yeerk pool.

"No!" she screamed. With one violent wave she shook me from her hand.

<Ahhh!> I clutched wildly at the stone face of the balcony wall. Amazingly my talon caught on something. About three feet down. And with weak, broken fingers I grasped a rough, small protrusion. My heart hammered.

"You little . . ." She strained to reach me. To knock me off and send me careening to the cavern floor. I was just beyond her grab. It was a matter of seconds now. That's how much longer I could hold on. My fingers were slipping. I was heavy. I was running on nothing but adrenaline and that would give out in . . .

"Rrrrrooowwrrr!"

An enraged roar. A roar I recognized.

Taylor started to turn, but too late.

Two brown claws closed over her shoulders, pulled back before she could scream. I heard a thud and I knew she'd gone down hard.

A grizzly bear claw reached over the balcony, gripped my back, lifted me up. Taylor lay incredulous on the floor. I focused on finishing the morph to Andalite.

Rachel's mass filled the balcony. She began to growl. Deep, continuous.

She picked the sub-visser up off the floor. Taylor struggled, but without result. Rachel's grip was unwavering, strong. She bellowed an animal cry of retaliation.

For a split second, time froze. And I saw Rachel and Taylor face-to-face. One strong. Her morph a crazy manifestation of an inner strength and bravery. One weak. This girl for whom appearance had been everything, honor nothing. This poor girl whose weakness had made her easy prey for the Yeerks. And I felt pity. Pity for my torturer.

Rachel's claws closed on Taylor's neck. Crushing her esophagus. She was turning blue, suffocating.

"Help!" she rasped pitifully. "Someone help me!"

<Rachel! No. Rachel, don't do it!>

<She dies, Tobias. For what she did to you, she dies.> She moved as if to slam Taylor against the wall.

<No!> I yelled. <Rachel. No.>

Rachel turned to look at me. Hesitated. Then dropped Taylor like a crumpled candy wrapper. The sub-visser fell to the floor and scrambled for the door.

<You know she should die, Tobias,> Rachel said.

<She will,> I said. <This is the Yeerk who lost a prisoner. Leave her to Visser Three.>

<What she did to you . . .>

<Rachel. Be Rachel, not her.>

# CHAPTER 27

It was a windy day. Sunny. We were all there, all but Rachel who'd had something to do with her dad.

We were all in human form. Even Ax and me. I sat on the sand at the beach. The breeze whipping my hair. The waves racing up the shore.

Ax was sitting next to me, unpacking a kite he had made out of scrap wood strips and paper bags. Untangling the string. Preparing for a test flight. A human hobby he said he found unaccountably peaceful.

Cassie was down nearer the water, scanning for any injured life.

Jake and Marco were playing catch, forcing levity. Jake rocketed a flawless spiral through the air.

"Ax?" I said.

"Yes, Tobias?"

"I had a lot of hallucinations back there. A lot of crazy visions." I tried to keep my tone casual. I paused. "But there was this one. It was just so real. I mean, as real as if I had lived it. It was Elfangor."

Ax looked up from his work. He stopped fussing with the string.

"A series of memories so intense. I was drowning in pain, Ax. I really thought I was dying . . . and then, all at once, I felt the icy cool steel of a tail blade against my forehead and I . . ."

Ax made a sort of gasping sound and dropped his spool of string. His eyes were wide with a startling intensity.

"A blade? Against your forehead . . ." He trailed off, his voice quaking with surprise.

"Ax. What?"

He was clearly disturbed. Like I had just shaken his reality. The wind began to drag his kite across the sand. He didn't care. Just sat there, absorbed in his thoughts. I ran after the thing and brought it back to him.

He shook off whatever it was and regained his customary composure.

"No," he said, more to himself than to me. "It's all nonsense, of course. We are a rational people . . ."

"What is it, Ax-man?"

He started hesitantly. "A legend. A spiritual rite, really. *Utzum*. Certain medicine men believed they could pass memories through DNA. Legend says these memory messages are triggered by imminent death. A surge of strength during the last moments to ease their passage. Ancient superstition."

"Yeah. You're probably right. Just a hallucination," I said.

A flash of gold. Way down the beach. A tall, graceful form pushing over the dunes to meet us. Rachel!

I jumped up. Ax was back to work on his kite, muttering something about thick, clumsy human fingers. The others all now engaged in a game of Frisbee that seemed to involve a lot of splashing.

I started to run toward Rachel. She saw me and smiled. I slowed as I neared her, breathing hard.

And suddenly I had my arms around her. I buried my face in her hair. She held me tightly.

"Bad," she said.

"Yeah," I whispered. "Real bad. I came close to, you know. Awfully close. I was so . . . I mean, I didn't . . ." I took a couple of shaky breaths. "I lost myself. Didn't know who I was. Not sure I do now."

"Tobias," she said quietly, "I know who you are."

A long, long time while neither of us spoke. Neither of us moved.

Then, she said, "Hey, it's nice and warm. But there are some killer thermals."

I smiled. "Let's fly."

"Yeah," she agreed. "Right after I do this."

She kissed me.

"Okay, now let's fly," she said and laughed her wild, wicked, self-mocking Rachel laugh.

And in a short time we were coasting on a thermal, high over the beach. Over the distant hills. Over the city. Over everything.

The memory of the mission was far behind. The close call with death forgotten. For a while.

Who am I? What am I? A bird. A boy. Something not quite human. Something more than human.

The person Rachel loves.

I discovered something amid the pain and terror and confusion. I discovered that the answer to what I am, to who I am, isn't something to be answered in a single word or a single moment.

It could take a lifetime to figure out who I am.

For now, I'm willing to hang in there, floating on a thermal. Biding my time.

## #34 The Prophecy

Three days had passed. Three days of having the strange, sad secret Andalite-turned-Hork-Bajir in my head.

Sleeping with her on the hard, cold deck. Awakened shaking, sweating, wanting to tear my head open with my bare hands as I felt the awesome grief of her nightmares.

Eating with her, if you could call the concentrated nutrient pellets food. Going to the bathroom with her. A lot more togetherness than I'd have preferred. Bad enough figuring out how to pee in a toilet designed for Hork-Bajir. Worse doing it with an audience in your own head.

We had gotten good at sharing control of speech. I controlled everything else. I had gotten used to it. I still didn't like it.

The Arn had stayed at the helm, ignoring us

for the most part. I'd learned nothing more about him. Was this really some voyage of redemption for him? Aldrea doubted it. And she knew a hundred percent more about the Arn than I knew.

Jake was talking with Quafijinivon when we translated out of the blank white nothingness of Zero-space into what now seemed to be the warm, welcoming black star field.

The Arn checked his sensors.

"Quafijinivon says we are now in Hork-Bajir space. We may pass the Yeerk defenses unnoticed. Or not," Jake announced. "We should get ready. We don't know what we'll be walking into. I want everyone . . ."

Marco held up his hand like he was asking a question.

"Yes, Marco."

"Do we have correct change for the tolls?"

Jake blinked. Then he grinned. He and Marco have been best friends forever. Marco knows how to knock Jake down a peg when Jake starts taking his fearless leader role too seriously.

Jake sat down on the floor across from me/Aldrea.

"I don't see why we couldn't have gone Z-space the whole way," Marco whined.

Ax and Aldrea both laughed. Then they realized they were both laughing at the same thing and they both stopped laughing.

"Just say it," Marco told them. "I am but a poor Earth man, unable to understand the ways of the superior Andalite beings."

"Hork-Bajir," Aldrea corrected him.

<Aldrea, why do you —> Ax began.

A flash of green streaked by.

"Shredder fire!" Aldrea yelled, and suddenly I was up and running toward the front of the ship. She had taken control of my body! It was so sudden, so effortless.

Ax reached the "bridge" first. He leaned his torso forward and looked over Quafijinivon's shoulder.

<One of ours,> Ax said. Then he clarified. <An Andalite fighter. It must be on a deep patrol. Harassing the Yeerk defenses.>

"Can we outrun him?" Jake demanded.

"They're between us and the Arn planet," Quafijinivon answered. "We're smaller. It's possible we could outmaneuver them. But it would place us well within their firing range."

Tseeeeeew!

The Andalite fired again. A miss! But the cold, hard data from the computer made it clear exactly how close it had come.

"Fire back!" Rachel burst out. "Knock out

one of his engines or something. Enough to keep him busy until we can land. They can't follow us down."

Quafijinivon's red mouth pursed thoughtfully. "Young human, that pilot is an Andalite warrior. One of the best trained fighters in the galaxy. I cannot hope to win a battle with him."

Ax and Aldrea both said roughly the same thing, which translated to human vernacular was, <You've got that right.>

<We can't fire on an Andalite,> Tobias said. He was flapping a little nervously, being tossed around as the Arn swung the ship into an evasive maneuver.

"So we let him shoot us down?" Rachel demanded. "There's one of him, seven of us. Or eight."

The Andalite fighter was coming back around in a tight, swift arc. In a few seconds his weapons would come to bear on us.

"Ax?" Jake asked.

<I cannot fire on a fellow Andalte who is merely doing his duty. Do not ask me,> Ax pleaded. <Maybe I could communicate —>

"No!" Aldrea interrupted. "If the Yeerks pick up a voice transmission, we're dead. They'll vector everything they have at us. We'll all be killed and so will the Andalites."

"Here he comes," Toby said.

I looked — and my stomach rolled over.

The Andalite fighter was on us. Seconds from firing.

This time he wouldn't miss. . . .

# ANIMORPHS

# Cassie is losing her mind.

But she's gaining the mind of another. Aldrea. Friend of the Hork-Bajir. Daughter of Seerow, Andalite Prince.

Aldrea died in battle, but her *Ixcila* survived. Her persona, her memory, and a valuable bit of information now belong to Cassie.

This *Ixcila* is powerful, but is Cassie strong enough to use it?

# ANIMORPHS #34:
# THE PROPHECY

## K.A. Applegate

**Coming to bookstores this September!**